THE DAUGHTERS OF CARRAWBURGH

NIGEL PLANE

THE DAUGHTERS OF CARRAWBURGH

Matador
9 Priory Business Park
Kibworth Beauchamp
Leicestershire LE8 0RX, UK
Tel: (+44) 116 279 2299
Fax: (+44) 116 279 2277
Email: books@troubador.co.uk
Web: www.troubador.co.uk/matador

ISBN 978 1780881 218

British Library Cataloguing in Publication Data.
A catalogue record for this book is available from the British Library.

Typeset in 11pt Minion Pro by Troubador Publishing Ltd, Leicester, UK

Matador is an imprint of Troubador Publishing Ltd

Printed in Great Britain by the MPG Books Group, Bodmin and King's Lynn

To Pat, with love and thanks

Prologue

The infant curled up on the settee in the sitting room so that his knees nestled against his stomach and the blanket enveloped him. As he gazed into the warming fire, the patterns of the red and orange flames dancing among the glowing coals transfixed his gaze. The awful, intense ache in his tummy was at last easing, and the tears caked around his eyelashes were beginning to dry. The soothing warmth around him made him feel safe again, and he could hear his mother not so far away in the kitchen, gently humming a lullaby.

He was wide awake now after his ordeal, and so his young exploring eyes and mind began to wander from the fire, and to the floral multicoloured patterns of the blanket material, all rough against his skin. They seemed to dance and shift about in the orange glow, right in front of him. His gaze moved on to the elaborate mock Georgian wallpaper with its intricate regal patterns, and then back to the fire again. He absorbed every detail in the ever-changing shapes and movements like no grown-up ever could. The gentle tick-tick of the clock on the mantelpiece made him feel warm as he waited for its tuneful chimes to comfort him.

Suddenly a faint creaking noise came from the ceiling high above him, and his wandering eyes froze. He looked up at the cracks in the plastering, but the 'creaking' moved down to the patterns on the wallpaper, and it grew louder and seemed to be all around him. The patterns became larger, then smaller, blurred, then focussed, then blurred again until all of a sudden they vanished.

The ceiling had given way and exposed a dark and thunderous sky, with rain clouds that threatened him over the open canopy. A bird, black and silhouetted, circled in the greyness overhead, with its wings stretched and its cruel hook of a beak poised. It swooped towards him, and made him flinch as he cried out.

The creaking noise in the walls all around him grew so intense, until they cracked and splintered, and formed into huge stones. They stood tall and imposing over him, against the shimmering grey and cobalt-blue sky. The creaking noises faded into whispers, barely perceptible at first. He couldn't hear what they were saying, but the whispering grew louder…many, many voices, coming from within the stones that loomed over him.

"Mummy…Mummy," he screamed.

But Mummy wasn't there. A sweet fragrance filled the air, one that his young mind didn't recognise yet. The ticking of the clock grew louder and heavier as it took on a life of its own. Its animated form leapt from the mantelpiece towards him until it transformed into a tower of stone, so tall and dark against the sky. Another voice whispered from within its walls and a lady dressed in black with long, funny, spiky curls of hair to her waist appeared at the top of the tower. For a moment his cries ceased as he gazed with his trusting, infant eyes into her face and into the large eyes that beckoned him. He yearned for the curves and softness to embrace him – just before the feeling of horror –

It wasn't Mummy. She wasn't there.

The bird swooped from above like a plummeting sword… a short, stabbing sword.

He hid his eyes and cowered under the blanket. His cries became louder and desperate:

" Mummy…Mummy."

Just then his mother emerged from the doorway wearing a worried frown. She leaned over him, puzzled.

"What's the matter little soldier? Has the tummy ache returned?"

*"The noise in the walls...the creaking..."*he stammered.

*"It's alright, it's just a bad dream,"*she smiled tenderly, as she stroked his forehead.

Sam Layton was only two years old but, as he was later to realise, these were no dreams; they were visions…communications from the other side with his open, innocent mind acting as a receiver.

And they would recur…again and again.

With increasing despair, his mother had sought the help of doctors, specialists, and carers. Then the man came – tall, with a long black coat and dark eyes that flashed when they caught the light, though he couldn't remember the face. The man never looked at him or acknowledged him but he knew they were talking about him – the man and his mother, as he looked on from the sitting room and into the kitchen.

The man spoke slowly and concisely, though he never understood the words, which were soon forgotten to him, but his mother acquiesced to whatever the man was saying, and she seemed sad. She no longer sang.

But the more the man visited, the less frightening the dreams became. Sam just accepted them.

Then the man, or his 'uncle', for his mother would describe him as that and no more, visited less and less. His mother became strong again – the way he, or any child would want. By the time he started school, it was all but a forgotten affair.

Yet the visions would still recur and haunt him when he least expected. He tried to tell them – the grown ups, then his friends, but the rebuff always came down to the same accusing question:

"So how long have dead people been talking to you?"

First it came from the bullies in the playground, then from the idle teenage curiosity. Friends came and went, and so did the girls. No one wanted to get close to him, and it was always the same:

"I don't understand you," they all seemed to say. "Why would an affable and dependable fellow like you, with that winning smile, and who would go out of his way to help anyone, want to get mixed up in all that sort of thing?"

Or, "I'm very sorry Sam, you're such a sweet guy, really you are but..."

But the recurring images – the raven, the sword, the megaliths and the tower, as well as that fragrant smell of jasmine would return to him less and less as he grew to manhood, and to the point where he no longer feared them.

Yet the gift to 'see beyond' as he saw it remained.

Now he was no longer mocked and bullied. Now when the bereaved and the hopeful came to see him during a session at the Spiritualist Hall, or after private sittings, they thought he was wonderful – a performer of miracles!

And it was true, judging by the tears of relief and joy streaming down their faces, and the shake of their hand gripping his. It was as if their newfound euphoria and strength had released them from a terrible, yet untold burden of grief and despair. And he felt it too; quite often the tears would start, as well as a lump form in his throat. An exchange of smiles with the grateful soul in front of him would occur, like a golden sun emerging after that dark rainstorm from long ago as he lay on the settee.

He never hardened and he seldom failed his clients.

Summer

1

Fleur slumped to the ground, fighting for breath. The earth and the gravel jabbed and cut into her flesh like shards of broken glass. She knew she about to die, but she was exhausted and could run no more.

She placed her hand on the gash that ran along her thigh. The blood, sticky and congealed, mingled with the dirt that had stuck to her hands as she lay on the soil inside the stone cairn. The stinging pain from the wound tormented her.

What a mess she must have looked: torn stockings, feet cut to ribbons, and her long, fair hair, all matted, soaked and coated in grime, only a day after she'd had it plaited into twisted ringlets just as they had instructed. Somehow she forced out a bitter laugh; still thinking of her vanity as though it still mattered. Then she cursed and wept at her misery and despair – to die so young and to end her days like this in the numbing cold and inside a stone tomb of all places.

She rested her head against the hard stone of the chamber wall. Behind her, a dark void led underground, concealing who knows how many similar alcoves that once contained the bones of the ancient dead. Ahead lay the entrance and the faint outline of the open dull blue-grey evening sky. It was too much to hope the approaching twilight would conceal her.

How had it come to this? Just an hour or so before she had been infused with her usual self-confidence and completely in control of her own destiny. She knew the dangers but could always tell how to recognise them and when to get out. She had learned from others in her trade. An hour's pay she was told, and good money too. It would involve the usual, and role play probably, but she wouldn't even have to go all the way – just act out a bizarre but harmless fantasy Megan had reassured her.

Yes it was all down to Megan, this was her fault, and she would never have met her had they not been mutual friends of Emma, the archaeologist. Fleur liked hanging out with Emma and all her colleagues from the university. It was a good way of introducing her to all those wealthy academics – in Fleur's mind a rich source of potential clientele. But she'd actually begun to look upon them as friends – especially Emma; perhaps there was a better way in life after all. She cursed again; she had been foolish and naïve. She hadn't followed her mother's advice of trusting no one.

It was through Megan that she and Emma had been introduced to the owner of the house on the fells. By all accounts he was an aloof and somewhat mysterious man, but nevertheless wealthy, and he got them both work – though by their different professions of course.

Yeah, just an hour's work Megan had said. A rather oafish and sullen looking chauffeur who never spoke a word had driven her to the hall in a limousine, completely alone. Gunter, she thought Megan called him. She helped herself from the drinks cabinet, after all, she took pride and satisfaction in what she did; she was providing a service she told herself. Besides, it helped steady her nerves.

The car eventually drew to a halt beside a tall and somewhat grand entrance hall, with towering ornate pillars of stone. This was the big time. Megan was there to greet her and continued to reassure her, especially so when she silently gestured for Gunter to disappear. She was ushered into a spacious, dimly lit sitting room and then promptly left alone as Megan closed the doors behind her.

It wouldn't be long now.

She helped herself to another drink from the cabinet, stripped as previously instructed and put on the white knee length gown that had been provided. She wasn't sure what to expect but somehow the robe seemed to compliment her hair, arranged in long spiky plaits earlier that afternoon. She left on her stockings – well just in case as that never failed. A thousand pounds Megan had said, maybe more. This was it, the big time; if he was nice, if he was to be a regular client, then soon she could quit all of this and perhaps get an education – Emma would show her the way. Perhaps her mother was wrong. She'd find her again and tell her as much. She'd ran away from her at fourteen.

A grandfather clock ticked slowly and inexorably from the corner of the room, the only thing breaking an eerie silence. She might as well make herself comfortable while she waited. She slumped into the plush armchair by the open fire, the glass still in her hand. Only dimly lit wall lights and the flames from the coals in the hearth lit the room. They cast a reddish glow on the antique furniture and chattels all around her. A medieval suit of armour, swords, shields and coats of arms that filled the walls surrounded her. In front of her, the French windows, slightly ajar, overlooked the fells, themselves awash with an orange-red hue from the setting sun. A mahogany writing bureau stood before them, stacked with seemingly ancient scrolls and open leather bound tomes.

She stepped over and glanced down at the ageing cream pages. She frowned, the drawings were in modern hand – geometrical circles and shapes, and perfectly drawn lines and labels such as 'sarsen', 'portal', 'ritual' and 'sacrificial', words which meant nothing to her.

The heavy chime of the clock made her start and extinguished the silence. She dropped the glass as she turned around. Her client had entered from the hallway. He was tall and dark, and the light from the room reflected in his pupils. Such darkness. For a moment, it stirred a distant memory…

The musty smell of earth and dampened gravel bore into her nostrils, inflaming her sinuses. The sweat from her body seeped through the grimy gown – the only thing keeping her nakedness from the night air and the cold. She wept. If only she had run at that point, when she still could…

But his smile, almost benevolent, even paternal, had disarmed her. He spoke articulately and yet softly. He called her by her real name, not her working name. How could he possibly have known? Unless…

Given time, she would have remembered.

But then he was on her. He grabbed her by the wrist and pulled her towards him his speed and strength overpowering her. Then he spun her around, her head and throat caught in a vice like grip by his arm. A flash of a silver blade in his other hand from the corner of her eye told her all she needed to know. She'd have one chance and no more – the pepper spray can still concealed in her stocking top – one brief moment with her free hand that's all – if she could only…there –

The short hiss of the spray led to his squeal of agony. His grip loosened and she fell to the floor. He twitched and writhed as he clawed and gripped at his face, and yet, in a state of shock, all she could do was stare at his hands and the long fingers with the large cygnet ring that hid his face.

But she came to her senses, and bound through the open French windows. There was no time to think, or to plan; all she could do was run…run down the lawn, through the flowerbeds and onto open land. Her feet, naked and cold, became scratched and torn, and they bled. The slightest twig, stone and bracken from underfoot dug into her and she began to slow. She glanced behind her; there was no sign of her pursuer; he was probably still lying there, blinded but angry. If she could make it as far as the woodland maybe she could hide, wait until dawn, and then find a road. Yes that was it; best not to panic, but to plan with what cards she had been dealt. She still had breath in her body. Yet if she had time to think, she would have realised what painfully slow progress she made. Her feet were cold and cut to ribbons, and she could barely walk. They had all night to find her.

She reached the woods. Only a fence to climb…that was where she gashed her leg. She cried out as the splinter tore into her thigh, but it was too dark for her to notice the flow of blood, only to feel its warmth down her leg. She staggered and hobbled to the shelter of the trees, only to find a mere copse; a clump that overlooked a wide-open valley across fell land. She wept with despair.

But as she squinted into the fading light, she thought she saw what must be a road, or a track way, or something, right at the bottom. No time to plan; besides instinct wouldn't let her. She limped and hobbled down and across the open terrain but the pain became excruciating. She halted and glanced around again; still no sign of anyone. Maybe…just maybe she'd get out of this.

But only after a few more steps, the sound of a falling rock or stone from somewhere distant behind her made her halt in her tracks again. Frozen with fear, she succumbed to panic.

A few metres further and she came to a narrow, pebble-strewn pathway. The ground rose in a hump beside her, and then levelled out ahead as the earth and track curved around. There seemed to be an entranceway that led into the mound. She remembered Emma describing to her the numerous burial Cairns dotted around the landscape. Well, she could run no more; this was to be her hiding place, or her place of doom. Either way, she was so tired and she could go no further.

Her head throbbed, propped against the hard stone wall, and her hands felt sticky as the blood seeped through from her thigh and into her palm as it pressed on to the wound. Yet the pain had numbed into stiffness, so that her leg had become deadened and immobile. Exhaustion was beginning to take hold even though the other pain in her head seared. All she wanted to do was sleep.

She closed her eyes. Now she remembered the man from when she was a little girl, and the way her mother would go with him. Then she'd return, always with a present; a toy maybe, or a pretty dress. She was a child, she didn't understand, but now she did. She wished her mother was there now. She wanted to be that child again.

She heard the footsteps approaching the entrance, and then saw the outline of the man silhouetted against the twilight sky. It was Gunter; she recognised him by the distinct outline of his bald, ball-shaped head. He stepped over and lifted her frail body from the earthen floor with little effort. She was too weak to struggle. Her dead leg buffeted and dragged against the ground as he carried her purposefully along and into the open. Then he released his iron grip and she crumpled to the floor and at the feet of another man. His shoes, neat with tidy laces, filled her vision. She barely had the strength to lift her throbbing head and to take in the greatcoat and the leather-gloved hands. But it was too dark for her to notice what she imagined to be the redness in his eyes, or the vile retribution that burned from them – she was grateful for that.

She sensed another warm trickle running down the inside of her thigh, and she knew it wasn't blood. So she closed her eyes, just as his hands reached out again.

When she opened them again, she looked towards the valley below her, and to the tall column of stones as they stood in a ring far from the embankment on which she stood. A body and a pair of hands gripped her from behind, one holding her head, making her watch the dusk turn the megaliths grey, then black. They were the ones Emma had told her about but for which she had taken little interest as to their purpose.

Emma – the swat – the bitch.

She closed her eyes again, and this time she knew it would be for good.

2

From high upon the escarpment, Sam looked down in awe at the circle of stones, as the dying sunrays turned the megaliths from a golden yellow to orange, and then to a blood red hue. The evening air and breeze cooled and soothed him, as the sweat on his brow caused by the exertions of his climb, grew cold. This was the place to be. An air of peace and spirituality reigned up here, and it appealed to him.

The surrounding fells and the valley below seemed opaque in the evening light as a rose pink mist gradually turned to grey. Below, among the stones, the group of human figures became less defined in the evening light as they hurried to clear up their belongings – tents, tools, gadgets and associated ephemera – all hastily bundled into the backs of the trucks and vans.

The police cordon tape was torn from the poles and the masked men in their white boiler suits and heavy gloves lumbered into view. Like aliens or spacemen from the future, they explored and intruded over the stone-age setting.

Carefully they lifted the body bag and placed it into a van. Then, after a few more dull and barely perceptible mutterings that drifted over in the still summer air, the blue light and screech of the police siren shot through the void and made him jump. One by one, the vehicles started up with a lurch and protest of gears, and then scudded along the dirt track, before eventually disappearing through the gap on the hill line.

Now the air of timelessness, peace and permanence returned to the circle of stone. He sat crossed-legged on the ground and breathed in the evening air, but the tranquillity would last only for a moment when further muffled sounds of human voices broke the air. He turned around to the stone cairn embedded into the grassy and rocky bank behind him, just as the torchlight emerged from its mouth. He squinted in an effort to make out the outline of the figure that carried it. Its silhouette defined a tall, well built man, exaggerated by the rucksack he carried on his shoulder.

More by instinct, Sam held out his hand in greeting and put on his warmest, broadest and most affable smile – it seldom failed him in these situations.

"Hello, I'm Sam... Sam Layton."

The extended arm wasn't returned.

The stranger switched off the torch beam and Sam's vision grew accustomed, so that he could now distinguish the man's rugged face as it stared back at him accusingly, as though he was intruding upon something. The fading, pale grey light reflected in the man's spectacles and, along with the thick, greying hair tied back, added to his imposing manner. Sam became aware of a second presence – a smaller, slight figure huddled inside a heavy jacket as it emerged from the black mouth of the entrance.

"Paul Carter... archaeologist," the first announced, but with a momentary hesitation, which cast doubt in Sam's mind as to his credentials, "but if you're part of that lot down there – the police, forensics or whatever, then you should be on your way and let me and my team get on with our job. And if you're just a sightseer, or worse, a journalist, then I should remind you that you're on private land. Mr Forrester doesn't take too kindly to trespassers."

"I can assure you sir," Sam stuck to the most cheerful, and hopefully disarming manner that he could muster, "that I'm in the employ of Mr Forrester too. I will not interfere and you won't even know that I'm here."

"Doing what exactly?"

"Well..." Sam rubbed the back of his neck, something he always did when he felt a lack of empathy from people in front of him, "I suppose you would call me a medium. I'm concerned with the spiritual side of things – of the departed, recent or otherwise."

Sam waited for the rebuff. He was used to it after all, and it was one of the reasons he had developed his trademark smile, albeit a sincere one. Predictably, the scientist continued with his silent, studious stare, so he continued:

"Mr Forrester is as anxious to get to the bottom of the murder victim's identity and the whys and wherewithalls of her fate as anyone else."

"Come now Paul," a softer voice came from behind the big man and the slight figure, hitherto inert, stepped forward. "Let the poor man go about his business, he can do no harm."

The cooling breeze blew a lock of soft, fine hair so that it hid her face, though Sam was aware of a pale blue eye watching him from an otherwise small and featureless face in the fading light; that, and a tiny delicate hand from a heavy sleeve coming to rest on the archaeologist's arm.

"And how much is he paying you then for your amazing psychic powers?"

Sam felt his face redden at his brass-necked effrontery. He had lost the battle of showmanship.

"Not so much as us Paul, I suspect. Anyway, it's none of our business, which is why you should not ask such personal questions and let him be."

"Not very much then. So you're an idiot as well as a spook. Still, nothing surprises me about Forrester. OK, so you've a job go do…so long as you don't get in my way, we won't have a problem, will we?" He turned to the woman, "The sooner the mystery about the dead girl is out of the way, the better."

He turned abruptly towards the track way that led down the slope. "C'mon Emma, it's time we got back to our caravan."

The smile dropped from Sam's face. He realised at that very moment from the look in the woman's eye that all wasn't what it seemed; she looked uneasy. She glanced at Carter's retreating form, then stepped closer to Sam. Her voice dropped to almost that of a whisper, so that it sounded strangely muted in the silent evening air.

"You say that Mr Forrester employs you?" She seemed anxious.

"I suppose you could say that, yes."

"Mm, it's a bit far-fetched isn't it? You know, mediums, psychics and that sort of thing… hardly scientific. Is that what you're really here for?"

He noticed how her eyes studied him. Strange he thought; the imperceptible darting movements of the pupils, reading his thoughts, absorbing every minutiae and detail in a split second – weighing him up and assessing him.

Or attraction maybe? Could be. Reading momentary, fleeting thoughts from newcomers was part of *his* stock in trade.

Either way, it all seemed so vivid in the dusk-filled stillness.

"I am who I say." He gestured with open palms. "I'm not here to interfere. You won't even know I'm here."

"It's just that, well…technically Paul isn't supposed to be here. Forrester dismissed him a couple of weeks ago." She fingered the buttons of her jacket nervously. "Well, what am I supposed to do? Forrester makes me head of the dig in his place and then expects me to walk away from Paul; well he *is* my husband. How can I desert him? You…won't tell Mr Forrester, will you?"

"Tell him what?"

"That Paul's still here."

Suddenly, a curious mixture of awkwardness and coquettishness emerged in the form of a forced smile.

A feeling of disgust came over Sam.

"You don't have to justify it to me. Like I say, I'm not here to interfere."

A few moments ago, he'd liked the gentle face and the warmth of the smile coming from the slight figure in front of him, now she was using him. She actually thought he was checking up on them! 'A bit of a bitch' he thought, and just as he was about to confess that quite frankly he was terrified of Forrester. Now he checked himself. If he was to have the run of the place unmolested by the surly man disappearing down the slope, he should play her along a little. He suddenly saw an opportunity.

"Like your husband says…so long as we don't cross each other, we should be fine. In fact, if you could show me what you've found here… you know, artefacts, the archaeology and so on, it would help me in my work, and then I'd soon be on my way."

The forced smile slipped. She glanced to the ground. So the coquettishness was an act, he realised. Seeing this, the vulnerable side, his attitude softened.

"Look, let's help each other eh?" he said in a final attempt to gain her trust.

She looked up again, and after a moment's hesitation any awkwardness she had towards him dissipated.

"OK, agreed; come with us back to our caravan." Her cheer had returned. "We're pitched not far from the dig, and over coffee we can compare notes or something. After all, we both have the dubious pleasure of being employed by our lord and master, Forrester!"

The woman introduced herself as Emma, before she strode ahead and caught up with Carter. After a few muffled and undistinguished words exchanged by the two figures in the distance, she turned and gestured for Sam to join them. Well, at least the ice was broken. Curiously, she emitted what Sam took to be a playful chuckle, just as she linked arms with the big man as they headed towards the downward slope of the hillside. It echoed again in that odd way in which sounds are exaggerated in evening twilight.

Sam followed a few steps behind after having taken a final glance at the megaliths in the valley below. The darkening red of the sky had caused its tooth-like spiky structure to turn black.

***

Sam sat at the small table inside the cramped confines of the caravan. Paul Carter placed a mug of coffee in front of him. Charts, surveys and computer printouts littered the table, seemingly in no particular order. The woman, with her back turned, sat in the corner as she powered up a laptop perched on a tiny desk. Her fair hair, straight and yet untidy, tumbled over her shoulders so that Sam saw nothing of her neck or face. Beyond lay a tiny stove and a partition that, Sam guessed, sealed off the wash facilities and bedroom quarters beyond.

"Welcome to our palace." Carter must have noticed him looking around. He sat in front of him and proceeded to light a cigar. Its fumes immediately cancelled out the aroma of coffee.

"Don't forget Emm, I want those images emailed to the incident room in Durham straight away, we've wasted far too much time as it is."

"Of course darling, when I have I ever failed you?"

Sam didn't need to see her face to recognise an affectionate, almost gently mocking tone.

"And," she continued, "I know…I know, I've got all that cataloguing to do of the latest finds, but I'll be on it first thing in the morning my love."

For the first time, Sam thought he caught the faintest trace of a smile on the big man's face. Then he turned his attention to Sam as he exhaled a plume of acrid smoke into the confines of the room, narrowed his eyes, and returned to his studious stare of him.

"So…a medium eh? Whose spirit have you come to contact then, the skeleton we exhumed, or this rather gruesome body of a woman found here forty eight hours ago? Hey presto – we have a crime scene and it holds up everything."

Sam gestured with open palms again, "That's a mystery to me. Mr Forrester just called for me to be here, that's all…and a surprise to me I must say since he's made it clear over the years since I've heard about him that he despises me and my kind. It makes little sense."

A chuckle came from over the corner. "Not to me," Emma said as she continued to work at the keyboard. "He employs *us* to dig up his land and gives us precious little idea as to what we're supposed to be looking for. It's not just the circle of megaliths back there, there's all the cairns and barrows scattered over the fells that cover his land, not to mention the sections of Hadrian's Wall he owns, which were never accessible to archaeologists before, let alone the public."

Paul butted in. "You see, he and his ancestors have owned this land and the surrounding fells for generations."

"Yes Paul, and he's guaranteed us work for a long time to come, and enough money to fund your own future projects," she said as she turned the swivel chair around to face them.

"You mean *you,"* Paul acquiesced as he drew in another breath of cigar smoke, "But now this… this dead woman they've found… it's holding up everything."

He stubbed out the cigar in frustration.

"Do you think they're connected?" Sam asked. "The corpse and the excavated skeleton I mean?"

"No, definitely not. Look, it's a grisly murder, or a drunken act of sex gone terribly wrong. How should I know? Perhaps it was a call girl, lured or taken there of her own free will, but stripped naked all the same, and with her throat cut. It looks as though the perpetrator was about to burn the body before abandoning the notion. Maybe they were disturbed."

Sam shuddered and he sensed Emma doing the same as they exchanged glances. They both saw the irony in the use of the word 'disturbed'.

"What about the ring though Paul?" she said, her tone now more sober.

"OK, OK so a ring from antiquity was found on her finger similar to the one found on the ancient skeleton, so it could be a crazed copy cat killing aping some ritual from the past I suppose."

"How do you know that?" Sam asked

Paul shuffled his feet, looked at Emma, and then back to Sam.

"We...acquired it, the one on the skeleton... well sometimes we do 'acquire' artefacts," he said in a tone that tried to justify his action,

"*You* acquired it Paul It's you 'acquiring' things that's always been your undoing. I've got to somehow explain away its disappearance."

"Well...it's valueless, Forrester won't know, he shouldn't be so damned mysterious. Besides, we know exactly where it was found in situ, so we're not exactly destroying any evidence of history."

It was clear to Sam that Carter wanted to move on:

"As for the skeleton," he continued, "that's what fascinates me, because we just can't put an age to it until the carbon dating results arrive; it's position just doesn't correlate to the time lines of the surrounding earth samples. It could be from as recent as Roman times, or date back to the late Neolithic and early bronze age, which was about the time the henge was constructed and the megaliths erected."

Emma frowned. She seemed anxious again and came over to the table and sat beside Sam.

"What Paul's forgotten to say is that although the skull was missing from the skeleton, we know that it was a young female by the shape of the pelvis, and there was evidence of burning around the pit where it was discovered, so this contemporary body *was* a copy cat killing, or some mock bizarre ritual…it's *horrible!*"

She leant forward and placed her hand on Sam's sleeve and studied his face. For the second time he noticed intensity in her blue-grey eyes as they bore into him. Again it sent a tingle of excitement through his consciousness.

"And we're all under suspicion you know," Carter added, oblivious to Sam's new interest. "Us, the team, even you Layton if you choose to stick around long enough. You…won't be around a great deal longer…will you?"

Emma's mood lightened once more at Carter's last unsubtle remark, and she leaned back again and reached for a mug of coffee.

"All except Forrester, he's untouchable…friends in high places. Bit of a recluse you know…I hear he spends most of his time in his home up on Cragburn Fell. You can see the Hall over in the hills when the sun is in the right direction."

"A collector of rare finds and artefacts," Paul added,

"that, I suspect is what all these digs are about. Truth is, I've rarely had communication with him, and it's always through third party agents and so forth, drawing up terms of employment, that kind of thing. I hear he's in to ancient books, and mysticism as well."

"Ah, well that I'm aware of," Sam intervened. "You see he makes himself well known throughout my fraternity…he considers us fakes and rogues, writes derogatory articles and gate crashes our meetings just to ridicule us…which is what puzzles me. Why does he want me here?"

Sam thought for a moment before continuing:

"I'm like you, I suppose, in that I've never actually *seen* him face to face; it's always been from a distance among a sea of faces, and across a dimly lit and crowded hall. I can't actually tell you what he looks like. How odd…

"All I received was a handwritten letter, asking me to 'attend the Daughters of Carrawburgh stone circle, to assess the recent disturbances there. Your usual fee, plus a substantial bonus will be paid upon the appropriate results'."

He reached for his jacket pocket and placed the letter on the table in front of them. Carter read it quickly and passed it to his wife before rising from his chair abruptly.

"Well, you do what you like. We've a very early start in the morning Emma, so I suggest we turn in."

"But we can't just throw Mr Layton out into the night darling."

She turned to Sam with a warming smile, "Come on, I'll give you a lift back to Wraxbridge, I presume that's where you're staying?"

***

Small talk wasn't Sam's forte. Not on a one to one basis and when unrehearsed (unlike a pre-arranged, personal spiritualist sitting) and definitely not, if he was honest, when he had an attraction for an unobtainable woman sitting right beside him. This, he knew, was a problem. If she had been a client, longing to get in touch with a loved one recently departed, he would be comfortable, and put her at her ease, and provide closure for her pain. And he prided himself at having 'the gift' to do so (not 'the power' as some described it.)

But, attractive though she was, with the pale blue eyes and the smile, all this would be lost on Emma, and her rather brusque husband. She was a scientist and everything was black and white. Ghosts? Spirits of the departed? Surely such notions would be nonsensical to her. What science couldn't demonstrate or prove didn't exist.

All this coursed through his mind as he stared into the headlight beams as they lit up the uneven terrain of the track way, with all its humps and rutted pits. Silence reigned. It seemed an age then, before they turned on to the relative smoothness of the B road to Wraxbridge.

Darkness continued to envelop them, save for the

luminous dials of the dashboard. The central lines of the roadway lit up one by one, captured by the light beam.

"So whereabouts are you staying?"

"Just in the town square. There's a holiday cottage attached to the antique and gift shop."

"Very nice. Paid for by Forrester I expect."

He felt himself blush, but he turned to look at her in the dark, and saw the warmth of her smile. He sensed it too, the teeth and the lips and the eyes and lashes in the quarter-light, and her pale reflection on the windscreen, the face and the long fair hair, free and flowing.

"I don't think your husband cares much for me."

She laughed. "I don't suppose you'll see us again. I, for one, spend much of the time researching and cataloguing the finds and working at Durham University. The facilities there are just what we need."

His heart sank. Stupid of him, he knew, but, curiosity had got the better of Sam. He wanted to know more about this couple.

"So…why," he asked hesitantly, "may I ask the change of role…you know…Paul seems very knowledgeable…so authoritative…why?"

"You mean why has Forrester given him his marching orders?" Her mood had changed again. "We met at Durham University when I was a student of history, and he lectured in archaeology among other things. I looked up to him, still do…he was, as you say, so knowledgeable, and confident as well. He was different from the students – they're fun but, oh I don't know, immature! Maybe Paul's a substitute father for the one I never knew. We're a team you see, as well as husband and wife."

She paused. "Why am I telling you all of this? Is this what you do when you talk to your clients – you make them reveal their innermost souls like this?"

Sam had no time to answer before she continued: "There was something of the rogue about him too, and it excited me. I knew he had connections with the bigwig landowner on the hill over there – Forrester – a great collector of antiquities, and he needed archaeologists… ones that break the rules if you see what I mean…"

"But I don't understand. Have they fallen out then?"

"Exactly. But I don't know why. And the dig still needs Paul. *I* still need Paul. No doubt all of this has affected Paul's temperament and his mood, but you shouldn't judge him; he's a very caring person with a wonderful sense of adventure. He's just a little fraught that's all, what with this awful murder… and Forrester wants results…"

There was angst in her voice.

"You seem worried," he ventured. "Can I help in any way?"

He realised the moment he asked, she might take his motives as not entirely selfless or platonic and that he was intruding.

"We're OK thanks."

There was a return to the silence and he continued to stare ahead into the darkness and the cats-eyes and white lines.

Eventually, streetlights appeared in the distance – tiny, approaching beacons of light, telling him that he was on the home straight.

Moments later, she pulled the truck up in the parking bay opposite the cottage in the square. It was late and the church clock struck eleven. But the shop light still shone over the cobbles, as did the ornamental light from the church tower opposite the square. It was a welcoming feeling.

But she still seemed edgy, as though something else plagued her mind, made worse by the stillness of night. Her face turned to him:

"Ever wondered where the name comes from – 'The Daughters of Carrawburgh' – Mr Layton?"

"Well, 'burgh' means settlement or town; it's common enough around here in the north…"

"Yes I know, it derives from the celtic language, but 'carraw' comes from a far older time. It could mean a pit, or a hole…"

"…From which sacrificial offerings are placed…?" He returned her stare.

The awkward silence returned, this time accentuated with fear.

"Well good luck Mr Layton, it's been nice meeting you," she said, formally.

An overwhelming feeling of disappointment hit Sam as he stepped down from the truck and onto the pavement. But just as he walked towards the door, with his back turned away from her, she called to him.

"Sam...take this..."

She reached out her hand from the driver's window and held out a folded piece of paper. He had just enough time to catch the serious look on her face before she wound the window up and spun the vehicle around with haste. As it sped away, the noise echoed around the bricks and cobbles of the empty town square.

3

Emma's scribbled note contained the words, *'Edwulf's Tower. Seek Megan's help'* and nothing more. He wanted to believe that there was more to this woman, with the pale blue studious eyes, hidden by the collar of her jacket and the long hair, than he first thought – more than just a scientist on a matter of fact mission. This 'cloak and dagger' mystery about her appealed to him.

Fortunately for Sam, there were plenty of history books and tourist guides of the area for him to learn a thing or two about the tower with the evocative name. Apparently it was the remains of a medieval fortified lookout post, or a Peel tower, as they were called. Built at a time when the rest of England began to enjoy a more peaceful and ordered existence, the Border country was still prone to skirmishes and raids by local warlords and gangsters back and forth across the disputed hinterland, because even when England was not at war with her northern neighbour, tensions remained high. Their motives, he had read, usually amounted to no more than that of cattle rustling and the stealing and spoiling of grain stores. Either way, they caused misery for landowner and peasant alike for three hundred years or more. He pondered over this as he sat at breakfast in the single ground floor room of the Georgian town house that formed the holiday cottage. Why hadn't she simply said it to him? It seemed that she didn't want to get any further involved, and didn't want Paul to know about the note either.

The sun shone through the large bay window, which overlooked the market square. Already, the noise of traffic and people sounded through. Voices came through from the adjoining shop. It was Monday morning, the height of summer and they were preparing for a busy day of tourists passing through and, hopefully frequently ringing tills.

The church clock from across the square struck nine and the BBC jingle of local news drew his attention to the TV set in the corner. It was, as Sam expected, like every day for the past week, almost entirely devoted to the body found at the stone circle. The images flashed from the departing contingent of police vehicles, to the police officer in charge, who's articulate voice was clearly designed to provide reassurance for anyone who needed it. He explained precisely that it was a one off incident, and they were pursuing the relevant lines of enquiry. An unnamed council official echoed this:

"There is no reason," he fidgeted and stuttered, "why holiday makers and traders should not go about their business and enjoy the fruits of the summer in Wraxbridge and the surrounding district."

A photo fit of the dead girl stared from out of the screen – young and pale, with a large round face and a small mouth with wavy, matted hair to the shoulders.

The eyes stared back at Sam, and stirred an emotion, perhaps even a memory, but it was so insignificant it vanished when the face of the reporter reappeared.

"She was," the reporter explained, "probably foreign; eastern European maybe, hence the difficulty in identifying her. Could a local employer help? If not, she was possibly an illegal immigrant, or maybe part of the sex trade. The police would follow this line of enquiry," the woman finished.

But in his mind, Sam had already resolved that there was nothing *he* could do. After all, Forrester's remit was quite vague. He switched the set off and set about the washing up. He supposed that he had been summoned there in order to pick up on any psychic vibes from the murder victim, so that afterwards Forrester and his archaeologists could get on with whatever they were doing. Any such vibes about the circle of stone itself and its ancient past would be too 'long gone' for him to sense, and he knew of no other genuine medium capable of travelling so far back. Besides, with the police and Paul Carter and his team of diggers anxious to 'reclaim their territory', he hadn't been able to get anywhere near.

No, he had decided. He was staying in this beautiful townhouse, in the picturesque, grey-bricked market town of Wraxbridge, at Forrester's expense. He would use the next few days to explore the surrounding area of Hadrian's Wall country purely as a holiday – damn the consequences. Forrester was out to 'get' him and his colleagues anyway, so why work for him? Promises of fees paid were worthless, he concluded.

But, as he cleared away the rest of the crockery and assorted tourist leaflets from the table, the note Emma had handed him wafted to the floor. He was about to crunch it up into a ball and toss it into the nearby wastebasket when he noticed a roughly scribbled diagram pencilled on the reverse side.

It puzzled him at first. It looked like a series of irregular shaped polygons that formed a circle, but in contrast, a neat set of straight lines came from them, criss-crossing and meeting at the centre. Then he realised – the irregular shapes formed a perfect circle – it was a diagram of The Daughters of Carrawburgh. Each polygon must represent a megalith, and each one was equidistant from one another. A compass point was also drawn on the paper, and one blob, to the northeast was marked 'missing'. On most of the shapes a cross was inscribed, and a key at the bottom simply labelled them as 'Burnt Offerings'.

He turned the crumpled paper again and re-read Emma's message. It was definitely written in the same hand as the diagram.

Edwulf's Tower beckoned.

***

The journey to the tower was straightforward enough – he just headed north towards the borders along the wide empty roads, and watched the scenery change from the largely sheep grazing pastures towards the purple hills on the horizon and the pine forests of Kielder. Once he had taken the correct turning off the beaten track, it was a simple case of parking at the most appropriate lay-by and heading off for a marked picnic area located in a small clearing within the forest.

All he then had to do was set off posing as a walker out on a nature trail along the pathways and clearings, which he knew, according to the ordnance survey map, bordered the private land he needed to cross. One fly-leaflet seemed to dominate the information board - a sketch of the dead girl, the same image from the TV screen; 'an artist's impression' it said, of how she may have looked when alive. It was more of a diagram really... a rounded face with large eyes, and wavy and plaited hair worn long, yet with a featureless, almost flat face that always seemed to be the case with these hand-drawn impressions. A desperate attempt to identify a lost soul. It haunted the deserted car park in the clearing, and it haunted Sam as he set off down the trail. There was, it seemed, the same stark piece of paper attached to almost every wooden signpost along the way.

A rusty wire with a broken style and a weather worn sign marked 'Private; Keep Out' was all that marked Forrester's territory - not even he had the power to restrict the inquisitive out here in the cool, dappled sunlight of the empty pine woods.

He stepped over the wire. By shielding his head and brow with his arm, he won the battle with the overhead twigs and bracken, and the jabs from the bramble as it somehow twisted around his ankles. It was then only a matter of moments before he emerged onto an opened grass meadow.

As he surveyed the scene, he realised that woodland enclosed the meadow on all sides except for a small gap on the skyline in the distant far corner - his next destination. Tempted though he was to traverse diagonally across the cooling and fragrant grass meadow for speed and ease, he was all too aware that he was trespassing. Concealed by a blanket of trees, the public track way and the road beyond may as well have been miles away, and there was every chance that anyone concealed within those woods would surely spot him.

As he skirted the circumference of the meadow, with the darkened shade of trees to his right flank, he had time to think. He had no idea what he was looking for at Edwulf's Tower, and it certainly had no bearing as far as he could tell on the mission Forrester had set him. All that was motivating him was a curious note which, if it had come from anyone else but the woman with the smile and searching pale blue eyes, he would have dismissed as melodramatic, even cranky.

But Emma came from a world of science, of exact reasoning, some would say of pragmatism and common sense. She was successful, confident and motivated in her vocation, and married and devoted to a man whose values and world she shared. She and Paul were, she said, a team. And Paul Carter would certainly have no time for *his* world of the spirits and the afterlife. No, it was a simple case of opposites attract and of the mystery of the female behind the veil. All he could have hoped for was curiosity, or at best, empathy from her; clearly there was something indefinable to him that she possessed and that he yearned for.

The aroma of the grass dew, still cool and wet in the shade of the trees by his side, soothed his senses and was the cause of his day dreaming, but then a sudden noise, a stirring from the leafy veil beside him, jolted him back. He froze and came to a halt. A cracking of twigs and bracken – footsteps?

Instinct made him crouch down into the grass and his eyes widened as he stared within. He reminded himself that he could easily be spotted out there by woodcutters, or farm hands maybe – this was working land.

The smell of freshly cut pine drifted through the air – there – just ahead, a gateway into the woodland, and newly felled logs, and beyond a sty, in fact a whole row of them, and a boar, or some such creature grubbing around on the forest floor, and the source of the disturbance.

He laughed to himself, and he was reminded that if he did meet anyone, then using his usual affable smile and bonhomie, together with his appearance of a rambler off the beaten track, he could talk himself out of anything, and simply declare that he was lost. Gingerly though, he walked past the stack of logs and watched as the pigs snorted and foraged around in their pen, minding their own business.

Onward.

The ground rose as he neared the exit of the meadow on the far side, and in the last few yards, he had no choice but to cross the grass towards the open skyline. Despite it being only a gentle rise, the sun beat down and he had to pause and rest when he reached the open gateway.

Beyond, the ground continued to rise, but in a broad vista of uncultivated meadow grass, with more pine forest flanked on either side. It therefore formed an avenue, which in turn formed his route. It ended at the top of the slope, where he could just make out a tower in the summer haze – Edwulf's tower it must surely be, and twenty minutes away.

But he sank to his knees as his breathing laboured and the sweat on his brow itched. He was so hot! A dull and distant, and yet distinct rumble of thunder put him on edge again. He craned his neck and looked into the sky. It remained deep blue, but over in the haze and towards the tower the sight of blackness seemed ominous. The clouds coming from over the horizon and seemingly from nowhere billowed like black ink diffusing in clear water. If he was to continue he'd better start, the sooner the better. Maybe there was shelter there.

He set off but his legs grew heavy and they ached.

Disturbances and undefined movements came from the curtain of trees either side of him and yet its cause remained invisible to him. The darkness swirled from within the woods like a whirlwind as the trees grew restless then agitated as they swayed - gathering momentum in the increasing maelstrom – an approaching storm? He felt the wind and a spattering of raindrops on his face. Overhead, the plumes of thunderclouds spewed from the still distant tower.

But he knew, right from that moment, after the second rumble of thunder, this was no rainstorm – at least not from the ordinary plane. This was different; this was what made *him* different and, at times like this, seemingly alone and helpless. It was OK when he was in a hall – at a meeting of like minds seeking answers and succour, but out here, in a rainstorm…

The thunder grew loud and threatening as the rain stung his face. The wind raged and the trees swayed angrily. And from the movements within came whispers and voices – indecipherable words, conspiratorial but then raised to agitation, and then shouting and anger.

The shouting led to screams of pain and despair. He covered his ears to block it out, and he felt himself shouting, for he couldn't hear his own voice:

"Stop and tell me what you want!" he yelled over and over.

The cry of battle, that's what it was. The clanking of metal and the blood curdling yells and cries made him realise; a throng of panic and calling from either side of him.

In his mind's eye, or on the psychic plane, he was never really sure which it was, he saw the forest melt away into open terrain. Figures emerged, white and opaque and ill-defined at first but rapidly taking on substance. Men and warriors in disorganised clusters, tightly packed, fought with clashing swords hand to hand. They writhed and they cursed. They growled and they cried in pain as one by one they fell to the grounded, blooded with the sound of swords ripping their flesh. Their ashen faces and their eyes, widened with terror, close to one another. He felt the panic and their heartbeat in his chest.

They closed all around him, but his reasoning – his *experience* – told him they could do him no harm; they couldn't even see him for they existed on the other side and he was witnessing a recording – a psychic display.

But it didn't stop him from being afraid and from feeling the despair of human suffering, and it hit him hard. It always did.

A voice seemed to be coming through; a clearer and calmer voice than the melee all around him. The forest began to reappear, blurred at first and swirling in the high wind, but eventually it re-formed and calmed to the sound of wood pigeons.

The storm was over. The wet grass glistened in the sunlight.

"Are you alright dear? You look all in."

A woman, in her sixties maybe, stood before him

with a curious look on her face. She was dressed in tweed and puttees and carried a walking stick. He was aware that he was sweating profusely and was in a state of distress. Yet he was struck by her odd appearance.

"I think you must have overdone it, walking all the way up here in this humidity." There was kindness in her voice.

Blankly, he looked behind him. He'd completed the walk up the grassy avenue as he hurried through the psychic disturbance and now he was suffering for his exertions.

"Come and sit with us for a while and rest." She gestured with the stick towards a wooden seat and to another woman of similar garb sitting there. "We're just about to take tea, would you like some?"

Sam looked around him as his breathing eased. He had reached the stone tower. It stood in a circle of mown grass, which formed a large clearing within the trees. Various walkways led off into the woods and a couple of benches lay strategically around the circumference of the circle. The tower was three storeys high and was rectangular in shape, with crenelations crowning the rooftop. A clock face was mounted on the near side.

Still dazed, he sat beside the two ladies and stared rather blankly at the tower in the centre of the greenery.

"Effie and I often sit here on a sunny afternoon and take tea," the woman with the walking stick explained, " but we seldom get visitors. Why are you here, young man?"

The sunlight cast an eerie glow onto her lined grey face.

"Oh just visiting the tower…did the rainstorm not… disturb you?" Sam faltered, still trying to shake the fog that lingered in his mind, and waiting for the reviving tea that never seemed to come.

"Ah yes…the tower," said the same woman. "Our late husbands had a particular fascination for that. It was built as a lookout tower against the raiders of the north…scene of many a pitched and bloody battle. It's hard to think of all that now because it's so peaceful here in this lovely setting don't you think?"

She gestured with the walking stick. Effie remained silent and motionless.

Sam thought of the psychic bloody battle and of the lost souls still there, and it deflated and depressed him.

"This land exchanged hands many times between the Reivers and the English," she informed him. "You should take a stroll over to the tower and take a look inside."

"Yes…yes I'll do that."

Sam stood up. His head felt fuzzy and he looked into the eyes of the seated woman still studying him. It was a kind smile and yet wrong – out of place. The other woman remained inert and there was no eye contact, and she looked down and away from him.

Yes, something was wrong. They seemed not to belong, dressed straight out of the nineteen twenties, taking tea. Besides, this was private land. What were they doing here?

Slowly he walked back into the sunlight and towards the tower, not really wanting to look back for fear of what he might see.

The oak door, located in the corner of the building, was heavy but as he pushed it open, he felt the urge to close it and leave what was outside behind him. Immediately, the loud, hollow echo of the ticking clock sounded in his ears. He was in a small, low vaulted, stone-bricked chamber, with sunlight filtering through several narrow portals on either side. In the centre, taking up most of the room, was the heavy working mechanism of the ancient clock – a series of solid iron cogs, wheels and pulleys leading up through the wooden rafters. The sound of their slow and methodical movement as they pulled and clanked bore into his head – and only that drowned out the heavy tick-tick-tick of a large iron bar and pendulum disc swinging heavily from edge to edge. It was a kind of slow torture as it echoed around the stone walls. It reminded him of a distant, indefinable memory – except now there was no lullaby to make it go away.

Wooden steps in the corner led him to the next floor. He took a furtive look out of a portal, into the sunlight and to the two old ladies, still sitting passively with a walking stick by their side. Were they watching him? Too far away to tell.

The room was similar to the last, except for two tiny chambers that led off and formed the hollow corner buttresses that supported the outer walls. The cables of the clock ran from the floorboards up through the rafters to the next floor. Still the echoes of the heavy tick-tick sounded in his head. He peered into the two chambers, no bigger than a few metres square. They were empty as expected.

Similar wooden steps led to the second floor. Up he went. It was the same as before, except that when he looked into one of the chambers, a crude and roughly hewn wooden table and a stone hearth furnished it. The smell of smoke and burning wood itched at his nostrils. The psychic playback was not over.

A dirty, mould-covered information panel lay broken on the floor, no doubt a product of when the tower was open to visitors, before it was swallowed up by the owner Mr Forrester. It explained that these rooms formed the living quarters of the men, be they soldiers or farmers, whose job it was to stay there for however long the threat of bandits or warlords who roved the area prevailed.

The clock continued to 'clank' both inside and outside of his head.

He crossed over to the other chamber, but the moment he entered an overwhelming feeling of claustrophobia and depression hit him, making him gasp aloud. He was only vaguely aware of a partition – a different wall to that of the stone – a wall in his mind's eye or imagination – before he reeled back as the despair overwhelmed him.

Some invisible force, so powerful, was preventing him from entering the tiny room.

Suddenly the clank-clank of the mechanism stepped

up a gear. Cogs whirled and cables moved, then the heavy 'bong' of the clock chime struck and sent him reeling. The panic that he had managed to suppress so far boiled over. Frantically, he scrambled up the last flight of steps and onto the open roof – anything to get away from the claustrophobia and whatever was watching him and controlling his mind down there.

But below him, he saw the Reivers – the fights and skirmishes, and the bloody cries again. The two inert figures on the bench began to dissolve, first their clothes, then their flesh withered, greyed then turned to dust and blew away in an unnatural wind.

So they weren't real either, not at least in the normal world, but he'd already guessed that.

He felt himself reeling, and it was all that he could do to steady himself and not topple over the edge. His head swam as he rushed down each flight of steps. He felt the invisible force push at him as he neared the entrance to that 'walled' chamber, but he had no time to think and was only vaguely aware of injuring himself on the thigh as he stumbled.

Down the last flight, through the door and onto the lawn, and past the withering figures on the bench, now no more than a pile of dust in the psychic wind, he ran and ran. Onward he continued until he reached the avenue of grass and towards the meadow, until, with his heart pounding, he could run no more. With a last desperate gasp, he collapsed by the gate to the field, and then blackness and silence engulfed him.

4

Sam watched as the golden lager, glistening in the evening sun, drained down Paul Carter's throat. The empty glass was placed on the table between them in a gesture that more was required.

"Very nice too, I'll have another," the big man said in expectation rather than anticipation, as a smile formed on his lips.

A few evening revellers were scattered among the tables, chairs and sunshades in the beer garden, which sloped down to a grey stone wall so typical of Wraxbridge. Beyond, the river Tyne, still in its youthful stage, flowed swiftly and bubbled its way under a yellow sand-stoned bridge. The water glistened with a deep blue hue in the evening sunlight.

Sam left, and then returned with two more pints of the golden nectar, as Paul liked to put it.

"So what's with all the cloak and dagger stuff?" Carter enquired. "I received a message from the local museum saying that you've been trying to get hold of my mobile number, so here I am! I never say no to a drink with friends."

"Oh, so we are friends then?" Sam was determined to out smile him, knowing full well this was a man where weakness of confidence was seen as a weakness of character and therefore an annoyance.

"Emma likes you, that's good enough for me. She's at Durham University researching on the excavations here, so she can't join us I'm afraid."

Sam felt his smile drop, not only because of his disappointment, but also because he was about to betray her confidence. Little did he know he would betray her in a far greater way in the future.

"So what is it then Layton? Spit it out!"

Another half glass was consumed. Sam thought he had better hurry:

"This…"

He handed Carter the note he had received from Emma with a distinct and uneasy feeling that it was never intended for his eyes – otherwise, she would have given it to him back in the caravan in her husband's presence.

Carter studied it for a moment and then handed it back to Sam with a dismissive gesture.

"Well yes," he explained, "these crosses mark the places where the remains of sacrificial victims have been found under each megalith. It seems to be Forrester's obsession – all he seems to want to know is whether we can confirm that such offerings exist under each and every one of the stones. Still…I can live with his whims, he pays well…"

But then he hesitated as he took the note from Sam again. "But I know nothing of this Megan, or of Edwulf's Tower, except that it's a fine example of a Peel tower. I don't know much about this Megan either, except that she's Emma's friend. Bit of an intruder really, always showing up. But why Emma should write this note to you...what's she keeping from me that's relevant to you?" His eyes narrowed.

Sam shuffled his feet, hesitated, and then asked, "How busy are you at the Daughters of Carrawburgh circle?"

"Very. The police have put us back several weeks."

"But I thought you're not even supposed to be there?"

"Oh I know it's only a question of time before Forrester's 'spies' realise I'm still sniffing around, so I've got to work fast. Anyway, sooner or later Forrester will realise he needs me again."

"You...wouldn't take time off to take a look at the tower? You know, geophysics, see what lies underneath, that sort of thing?"

"What?" Carter laughed out loud, "Hah! You mean, what lies beneath? Too many films, that's where your overactive imagination comes from! Some evil presence eh? The cause of your hallucinations and black out today?" He laughed again. "No chance buddy!"

Sam had lost out in the game of cool superiority and confidence, and his smile had dropped.

"What I experienced at the tower was quite real. I don't care how sceptical you or your kind are, I can't recall ever experiencing anything quite so intense before, especially when I think for how long I was out cold. It took all my strength and will to find my way back to the car. I'll go back alone if I have to, but aren't you the least bit curious as to why your wife handed me this note, and who this Megan is?"

Paul's mocking ceased and a frown replaced it. He pondered and then looked Sam in the eye as his smile returned: "For Emma's sake then!"

He rose and drained his glass.

"Come, we'll drive up there in my Range Rover, and I'll make an assessment. After all, Forrester did say that I could dig anywhere…but that's all I promise!"

"What, *now?*" Sam was exasperated.

"No time like the present buddy… can't hang around!"

As he strode across the beer garden and among the other drinkers and towards the car park, Sam struggled to keep up.

"Oh by the way," Carter said as he suddenly stopped and turned to face Sam, "This'll interest you - according to the lab, the DNA from that poor wretched girl who was murdered, matches the DNA that we were able to extract from the remains of the bones we excavated. Durham University concurs. They were closely related, now how weird is that?"

***

As they sped along the road north and into the forest, Sam couldn't help but notice there was a distinct cavalier approach to Carter's manner now – quite different from his attitude when they first met. Maybe it was down to the beer.

"We need to get there before sundown." Paul stated the obvious as they veered off the road into the picnic and car park clearing.

For a moment he paused with the engine still running. Sam was thankful that any remaining sightseers and empty cars waiting for their owners and dogs to return had left the scene. Evening shadows lengthened across the gloomy woodland and yet the white rectangular sheets posted on the fence and boards showing the face of the girl, still stood out in the fading light.

Paul studied the ordnance survey map.

"Look there, straight ahead." He pointed to a dilapidated gateway, "There's a bridleway. I reckon it'll bypass the spinney and meadow you described and get us on to the grassway that leads to the tower."

Quickly he alighted from the vehicle and strode up to the gate, and forced it open. They drove on with the potholes, bumps and ruts of the track way making them lurch in their seats.

"Rock and Roll!" Paul grinned.

Within moments they had turned on to the grassy avenue between the thickets of pines that Sam had trudged along earlier that day. The noise of the drive, along with the company of the ebullient Carter, kept away the demons and Reivers.

The Rover came to an abrupt halt on the lawn

outside the tower. Sam stepped down and groaned as he placed a hand in the small of his back. Still, it had been quick.

With the engine killed, the silence and the evening shadows rapidly closed in on them. A bright summer sky still shone directly overhead but it was fast turning a deep blue and most of the trees and surrounds were in shadow. The sun was low in the sky and the golden colours at the top of the tower were turning a sunset red.

"Are you alright dear? You look all in. Would you care for some tea?"

The voice from close by made Sam reel, but the two elderly figures were sitting on the seat some distance from them both. A glance towards his comrade told Sam instantly that Paul was totally unaware of the apparition, and then the stifling feeling of depression and despair he had felt previously returned. It was like an unseen force pressing at him, and the fading light seemed to make it more intense.

Paul reached for a backpack from the rear seat, and they set off for the entrance door. Paul looked at him, puzzled, as Sam gave the perimeter and the bench a wide berth.

The door opened with a labouring screech as it scraped the stone floor.

"It's the clank-clank of the clock mechanism... so heavy and slow... it's enough to drive you to despair," Sam muttered half to himself as he held his hand to his head.

"What?" Paul said, incredulous. "It's rusted through, look at it! That hasn't turned in years!"

Sam looked on in disbelief. Sure enough, a pile of red rusted cogs and coils hung limply and motionless from the rafters to the stone floor, yet the endless slow clank of the clock tortured his mind.

With a look of scorn, Paul switched on the torch beam. "I think I'll get a feel of the place first," he said disdainfully, and he disappeared up the flight of steps.

Sam stepped outside for fresh air and the oppressive feeling lifted, at least slightly. The apparitions over on the wooden seat had disappeared and curiosity replaced fear. He was regaining control, something he could always do in front of an audience, so why not here? He thought back to his infancy and the demons that spoke to him, and then realised that whatever had brought him here – Emma or otherwise – was for a reason.

Something, God knows what, was about to happen.

"Oi, Sam, look at this!"

Paul's very much real and down to earth voice came from within the building. He stepped inside and, quickly bypassing the rusty ironwork, ran towards the wooden steps.

"Second floor," Paul instructed.

Paul had entered the 'forbidden' chamber leading off the room. Sam stopped short of the archway as the oppression returned. He could only see flickering shadows within as flashes of torchlight danced around the enclosed space.

"A false wall…bricked up…making it even smaller. No wonder you felt claustrophobic," Paul said from somewhere within.

Sam peered in as best he could, but it was the 'unseen' wall fighting against him that caused him to cower away.

"Any fool can spot it," Paul went on as the light continued to dart back and forth into the darkness. "Elizabethan I think, judging by the narrow red brickwork, and the mortise is uneven... and rotten."

Sam heard the steady tapping of Paul's trowel, and then a momentary hesitation led to an exclamation of, "Oh what the hell!"

The torch was tossed over to Sam who only just caught it. He shone the light into the chamber only to see Paul placing his holdall on the floor and unzipping it. He withdrew a hand pick and mallet.

"Hold the light!" he commanded.

Immediately he began to hack away at the crumbling brickwork. The noise was deafening in the confined space, and dust flew everywhere.

"Archaeology it ain't. Indiana Jones it *is*!" he laughed as he manhandled the loosening bricks as they gave way.

Within a few moments the whole of the false wall collapsed, making Paul step back and stumble as they both let out a "Woo-ooh!"

The cloud of dust made them both cough and splutter. Sam, being furthest away, was the first to recover, and shone the light into the newly formed crevice.

Both men's eyes grew accustomed to the haze and gloom at the same time, and so both emitted a gasp in unison.

The grinning face of the skull silently screamed back at them, and then Sam dropped the torch.

"Holy shit!" Paul picked himself up from the floor and dusted himself down. They both sniggered as they regained composure, and Sam reached for the dropped torch and shone it towards the skull. Its hollow eyes and traces of dried and brown-wizened flesh reflected dull and morose, and the image bore into their souls.

But then a cooling, zephyr-like breeze brushed by Sam, making him gasp. The gasp grew to a convulsion as a silky wisp of hair brushed against his skin, just as a shape – a feminine form – it's outline black and curvaceous, seemed to pass right through him.

Stupefied, he turned in the direction she travelled, just in time to notice a swirl of disturbed dust particles on the steps leading to the rooftop.

"There!" he hissed and swiftly moved to the steps.

On the rooftop he had but a few precious seconds to take in the being watching him from the far corner – only a fleeting moment as he saw the silhouette of the curved female figure with bushy and spiky hair down to the waist - before it blurred, and then dissolved into nothing.

Slowly he made his way back down the steps and back to Paul in the chamber.

Already the archaeologist was crouching over the remains of the skeleton. Its brittle dryness was crumbling among the dust.

"Look at this," he exclaimed without waiting for an explanation for Sam's sudden exit. "Bindings around the wrists and ankles."

He prodded and picked with his trowel until the strands of rope crumbled away.

"And look," he shone the torch towards the skull, "just below the neck line, a clear and neat incision made by a knife. This was another sacrificial victim, bound and with it's throat cut to the bone. I wonder how many more I'm going to find scattered over these fells? "

"This?" Sam grimaced.

"Well, *she*." Paul stood up. "You can tell by the brow on the forehead and by the hips. This was a female."

The dust laden light beam caught the empty and hollow eye sockets and the gaping jaw. "Just a pile of dry and discoloured old bones…hard to think of it as a person really." Even the hardened scientist seemed touched by the suffering and sorrow it represented.

But Sam felt a sense of liberation. The feeling of depression had lifted and the heavy ticking of the clock had vanished – his ears and mind free and basking in blissful silence. He had freed the soul of this poor victim and now she could move on. He had seen her fly from the rooftop. This was the gift that he had given her.

But the silence was ripped apart by the sound of an approaching car. As it pulled up, the two men looked at each other, wide eyed and with a sense of unease.

They stepped onto the roof and peered over the battlements. A huge, blackened Range Rover boxed in

Paul's vehicle. A man stood in front, wearing a dark trench coat, and he appeared to be fiddling nervously with his gloves or his wrists, a trademark that Sam recognised. Two shorter but stockier men stepped out from the rear doors and they slammed them shut purposefully.

"Layton… Layton? Down here now!" the voice of the taller man growled, slowly and loudly.

Sam and Paul looked at each other with a feeling of resignation. There was no mistaking the presence of Forrester.

"It's possible he doesn't know that we're both here," Sam whispered. "There's no point in us both facing his wrath."

"Or worse…not a man I'd like to cross, just look at the size of those two apes he's brought with them. Are you sure you want to go down alone?"

For the first time Sam noticed a look of respect, almost humility from Paul Carter, and he smiled ruefully at him:

"No point in giving yourself away. You're in enough trouble with him as it is. No, I'll face this alone."

Sam's legs felt heavier as he descended the last flight of steps; no wonder they echoed around the confines of the stone tower. Best not to hesitate, he told himself.

He stepped into the night air. The tall, trench coated figure that was Forrester stood some way from the tower, with his back turned. The two thugs remained in the background and in the darkness, clearly designed to cut off any puny escape attempt by Sam. He thought it best not to even approach.

Forrester turned around. The car behind him, still had its engine running, and the lights on full beam, so that the face remained featureless and in silhouette. But there was no mistaking the flash of anger in the jet-black darkness of his pupils as the light caught them.

"Layton," he growled, but then he turned his face to the ground, and appeared to compose himself before looking across at him again. He still fidgeted with the wrist straps of his leather gloves.

"I ask you to perform a simple task…and to prove yourself, and yet here you are, off at a tangent chasing ghosts that are irrelevant to me, and on land that I haven't authorised you to visit." He shook his head. "Sam…you are just like your mother…"

He sighed, and spoke with a rich, eloquent voice, almost soft in tone that Sam knew, and felt he always knew from way back somewhere – even though he had only really seen him at lectures and the spiritualist meetings that he had grate crashed with a view to causing trouble. Yet, he could not actually *recall* him speaking at such gatherings; it was so strange.

The reflection of the lights glistened in his eyes again; his authoritative manner returned:

"You are required at the circle of megaliths, and I ask once more…did you sense the psychic energy of any souls contained there…ancient or contemporary?

Answer me, and I will pay you well!"

Sam hesitated and the silence felt endless, with nothing to break the quiet except the running of the engine. Finally, he bluffed by simply saying, "Yes".

The worst thing was, that the moment he said it, he knew Forrester wouldn't believe him. He waited for an onslaught of wrath, but instead his only reply was: "Very well," which he delivered in a very slow and calculating way.

Forrester turned back to the car and Sam let out a sigh of relief, but just before he opened the door, he turned to face Sam again and added:

"And you can tell Carter, skulking around up there, not to even think about taking away those human remains. That find belongs to me, and I shall be collecting it in due course."

5

Why had Forrester let him off the hook so easily? This was the question troubling Sam as he wandered around the grey-bricked cobbled streets of Wraxbridge the following day, and just before his next meeting with Paul Carter in the beer garden. Forrester knew he was lying; Sam hadn't even got close to the megaliths, let alone pick up on any psychic links there.

The sun beat down as he made his way onto the road south of the town and past the sightseers, who were steadily making their way back from the riverbank and to the car park. As he passed the souvenir shops and antique stalls, he wished he had taken up his earlier option of treating the whole thing as an unpaid holiday at the expense of Forrester, and to hell with the consequences. Instead, the visit to Edwulf's tower had posed more questions than it had answered.

To his surprise, Paul Carter was waiting for him at the exact same spot in the beer garden as before. The flow of water still rushed by in the peaceful idyll. Earlier in the day, Sam had idled his time away at the nearby remains of a Roman fort just north of the town, and one of several that flanked the southern side of the great Roman wall. There, in the mini-museum of finds, and to his surprise, he discovered a potted history of the tower. It seemed the foundations of the Peel tower lay on the remains of a Roman lookout post, built north of the wall to guard against earlier raiders – some fifteen hundred years before the Reivers. He looked forward to telling Paul of this little historic discovery, but he was already ahead of him.

"I know, and what's more, it dates back further than the Roman period. It was excavated in the nineteen twenties under the supervision of two amateur archaeologists; widows who were carrying on the work of their husbands who'd been killed in the Great War. It seems they found evidence of stone post holes proving that megaliths once stood there, and that they were situated on lay lines, which linked it to The Daughters of Carrawburgh circle, numerous causeways and barrows, and even Forrester's home up there on the fells."

Paul announced all this with a sense of triumph as he drained his glass and gestured for another.

"The trouble is," he went on, "like so many archaeologists of the day, none of this was written down or properly recorded… there was no systematic analysis of any of the finds and they disappeared, so you can only go on hearsay. Next thing, both of the two biddies had disappeared as well. Probably got bored I suppose, just a whim destined to be abandoned. Typical!"

He wiggled the empty glass so Sam left and returned with more of the sparkling gold. He was rather enjoying this, especially as the beer seemed to make this rather brusque man's attitude soften and open up.

Back at the table, Paul still had a look of triumph about him, and he pointed to a tiny box he had placed on the beer table.

"Open it!"

Sam found a small ring within, eaten by verdigris, and encrusted with dirt.

"Why, I didn't know you cared! I accept your proposal," Sam said with a grin. The beer was taking hold.

"Don't be stupid man! I took this off the hand of the skeleton last night."

"But what about Forrester?"

"Damn him! Besides, he wasn't expecting us to find it was he? But here's the thing… I've got to get it cleaned up and x-rayed of course, but I reckon it's pre-Roman… Bronze age even, which is about the time the stone circle was in use, and judging by the way the finger bone is stained, even melded to the bronze, I reckon that the skeleton was already ancient when it was walled up during Elizabethan times."

Sam's head felt fuzzy. "Evil at work," he muttered.

Paul ignored his remark. "Here's what'll interest you," he said as he re-pocketed the artefact, "during the time of the border wars…the raids of the Reivers, it wasn't uncommon for hostages to be taken by whichever side aspired to conquer, or re-conquer the surrounding land. They were held captive in the rooms of the tower. The prisoner would usually be a son or daughter of a nobleman or merchant or whatever, and, as long as the ransom was paid, they were released unharmed.

"Anyway, one account stated that a hostage held there claimed to have been 'spooked' by apparitions… faces of young maidens, appearing through the wall… and the chanting of pagans and so forth. Of course, nothing was ever written down, and over the ages the story has no doubt got twisted and elaborated, just like all ghost stories – *your* territory I expect."

"You don't have much time for me do you?" Sam was morose.

"Not at all… I wouldn't be here otherwise, drinking with you and telling you all of this. What will you do next?"

"Nothing! Absolutely nothing! Forrester seems to have obtained all the information he needed from you and your team – you know, the cremated remains underneath each megalith. Why he asked me to find out about any psychic links there I don't know…unless it is to expose me as a fraud. Well, I won't give him the satisfaction. I've spent the last two days enjoying the scenery of Wraxbridge apart from my adventure at Edwulf's tower, and," he gestured towards the bottom of the beer garden, the sunshine and the river, "tomorrow, I shall journey south and home."

"Home? What do you do for a living?"

"Quite normal. I'm a barber." Sam slurred and then frowned as he looked at his companion's thickset hair. "Looks like you could do with a wee trim yourself!"

Before he knew it, Paul had disappeared and then returned with a couple of whiskeys and with a quizzical look on his face.

"Aren't you at all interested to know who this Megan is?"

"Ah Megan. I'd forgotten about that…the note from Emma."

"Well I haven't. I shall be asking my wife about that one."

Sam felt a sudden twinge of hope, even optimism. She had confided in him by giving him the note, something that she had kept from her husband. Then, with a shaky wave of his glass, he said, "Ah Emma! I'll drink to that!"

But then his fogged mind told him to dismiss her as not so much as 'a might have been', but 'a never really in the running, and indeed spoken for' category.

"Here, take this," Paul said wryly, and he handed him the tiny box with the ring. "It's not valuable, I've seen them before and at least you'll have something for your trouble."

Sam raised his glass.

***

The sun had set. The babbling of the river still sounded but Sam had watched its deepening blue turn black so that all could be seen was the reflection of the coloured lights of the beer garden on its invisible surface. A curious sense of failure had overcome him. Failure over the megaliths and failure over Emma, now Paul, his unexpected drinking companion, had long gone. He sat in contemplation until the outline of the trees on the opposite bank blended into the night, and the air chilled him. Then he headed back to his digs.

He expected a heavy, booze fuelled and dreamless sleep, before finally heading for home around midmorning the following day…after he'd slept it off. He certainly didn't expect to dream.

But dream he did…or something.

He saw the widows. He saw their faces turn from a sun-kissed gold to an ashen grey. He saw them fall into the pits they had dug, along with their notes and their trowels, and the megaliths fall on top and crush them, until they too dissolved and formed into the tower watching over them.

He was aware of his presence at the great stone circle; it was so…normal.

How could it be a dream?

He walked among the megaliths clad in his boots and leather jacket, and he was aware of just how vast it was. And yet a cool and damp morning mist surrounded them. It bathed them in a diffuse, grey light. It hid their features, yet accentuated their shapes – tall and masculine, or smooth and curved, and yet still and silent… and cold.

He felt the cold and his mouth was dry.

Then… a sudden movement from over on the far

side – he wasn't alone; there was someone else... someone he felt, who belonged there. A figure emerged from behind – no – from *within* a stone, one of the smaller rounded ones. And then, just as in a dream, for this must be a dream, the stone disappeared, leaving the figure of a woman watching him; a beautiful, curvaceous being with long plaits of twisted hair into ringlets; a dark shape outlined by the misty backdrop

He watched as she moved on to the adjacent stone and embraced it for what seemed like ages, and then she moved to the next one and did the same. She held out her hand to them, and touched them, and then rested her head on them as if she were in some kind of bizarre communion. Each time she moved to the next one, she glanced towards him. He wanted to move away, he felt as though he was intruding, but he couldn't; he was mesmerised by her movement and the figure, so feminine.

He told himself that it wasn't real, but for sure, a psychic display contained within the stones was being played to him in his sub conscious. Something had brought her to life and made it all visible.

He felt for the ancient and disfigured ring Paul had given him and took it from his pocket. A fine coating of hair covered it and he felt it between his finger and thumb. He looked at it and noticed it twist into braided ringlets, and he knew it came from the woman.

She was now almost in front of him. How could that be? The tight tunic she wore and her pale skin made her look as cold as the stones and the mist, and yet she seemed unaffected by the chill. How could this be real?

She was upon him now – the figure, unmistakably wholesome and fecund, with the pale rounded face and the wide and staring eyes... and with the familiar hairstyle of long plaited ringlets.

She held out her hand and he passed her the ring. Her lips were slightly parted and she seemed to say:

"You DO have a link with those that dwell here..."

And as he followed her glance to the ground, he knew this was the place of the dead girl's final moments...

The sound of the shop doorbell's tinkle rang in his ears, shrill and startling; and then there was the sound of muffled voices as the shop next door came to life. He opened his eyes and squinted as the sunlight filtered through the curtains. The church bell jarred him, as did the roar of a car engine in the market square below as its echo amplified around the bedroom walls.

His mouth and tongue were parched and his head ached.

Even so, he would still have been away and heading for home considerably earlier had he not spent a frustratingly long and fruitless time searching for the bronze ring. He knew he had it when he arrived back last night, but now it had vanished beyond trace.

Autumn

6

From somewhere across the cobbled stoned square, a door slammed shut as the autumn gale whipped the fallen leaves into a visible whirlwind. Seemingly with a life of its own, it shot down the pavement and crashed into the stone wall. A dog, clearly disturbed by the commotion, barked ceaselessly from somewhere. Sam pulled the collar up from his jacket as the chill caused him to shiver.

He looked over in the direction of the noise and to the Georgian terrace of houses adjacent to the shop. His encounter there last summer seemed so long ago, and he smiled ruefully to himself at the thought that he should end his long spiritualist tour back here in Wraxbridge, and at the church hall opposite the very place that he had stayed.

Since then so much time had passed, and life had returned to the normality of the barber shop and of the meetings in the halls of the hopeful and the like-minded. But this *had* been a long tour, and as the weather turned, it only convinced him that he needed a break – just a little time away from all this – so when he climbed the steps that led to the entrance of the village hall that evening, he regarded the bill posted on the notice board with some relief. It simply stated that the spiritualist known only as Sam, who had become renowned and trusted throughout the north, would preside over this evening's meeting, but that it was to be his last audience for quite some time. "All were welcome," it announced.

The hall doubled as a theatre and stage, and as soon as he walked onto the boards the customary applause gave way to murmurings from the audience, followed by a hushed silence. The hall was packed with a sea of anxious and expectant faces, young and old. The lights cast a warm glow about them, and all thoughts of the howling autumn wind rattling through eaves and rafters were soon forgotten.

He felt relaxed at first, as he always did. His warm smile and the gesture of his hands, though part of the routine, were nevertheless sincere, and the people warmed to him. He turned his attention at first to the old widowed lady in the front row, then to the grieving parents behind her, and then to the lanky girl worried about her lost pony. Each in turn were touched by his words, his manner, and his amazing powers, as their tears of euphoria released them from grief. But even those among the crowd whose loved ones had not travelled through from the astral plane that night would not leave disappointed, because what they had seen convinced them that a world of the afterlife did indeed exist. That was all they needed to know.

Eventually the proceedings began to wind down. People were standing to leave, so he thanked them, took his bows, and wished them goodnight and god speed. After the gentle and prolonged applause, he walked towards the wings and, hidden from view, he watched the people as they slowly left the hall. As the crowd thinned out, he noticed the small figure of a woman remained. She was seated some distance from him, towards the back of the room.

She sat huddled in a large grey overcoat, which seemed far too big for her, and her face remained hidden behind its upturned collar as her untidy fair hair fell forward and hid her away.

A youth had begun to stack the empty chairs to the side of the hall, and as he edged nearer, his awkward glances towards her became more frequent.

"Show's over Miss. Time to go home," he said, eventually.

She sat there in silence and stared ahead.

The boy looked one way, then the other, not knowing what to do.

"Sam... Sam," he called.

Sam emerged from the closed stage curtain and immediately surveyed the scene. He walked towards her with purpose, but before he could say anything she spoke in a determined voice, but nevertheless it wavered with emotion.

"I'm sorry, I'm not usually like this, but I need to..." Tears welled up, and she choked, as her voice stuck in her throat.

He studied her for a moment, then after a pause, he spoke, "It's OK. What's your name?"

"Emma."

The voice shot through him like a bolt and he imagined the stupefied look on his face as his jaw dropped. The small, oval face with the pale complexion looked at him accusing and with incredulity as if to say, 'How could you not recognise me?'

The eyes no longer shone, was his silent answer, and it had floored him. Something was gone – the spark of optimism, of humour and purpose. She'd lost something – of course – she was grieving. This was something he dealt with all the time, his stock in trade, and yet he'd missed it.

"I'll help you if I can," he said in a confident tone that belied his feelings.

He turned to the boy, "Leave us and switch out all the lights, except the ones above us. I'll lock up."

The boy, only too keen to be relieved of his duties, did as he was told.

Sam pulled up the one remaining chair, and sat in front of her. With just an overhead light casting a pale white glow on their faces, the rest of the hall appeared to vanish. A cloak of darkness and silence surrounded them.

He looked into the face of the woman, but her eyes

lowered again as she looked down at the floor. She appeared to be trembling with grief and emotion, and he felt her resignation and sorrow deeply. This was so unexpected, such a shock.

Suddenly her eyelashes flickered, and she looked directly at him. The beauty of her moistened pale-blue eyes touched him, and he was all at sea, and as a tear ran down her cheek, the paleness of her skin seemed worn with sorrow.

"I'm sorry," she said with a forced laugh. "You're not exactly seeing me at my best."

He steeled himself; he had to remain professional. After all, his encounter with her before was brief and fleeting. And yet he knew that she was allowing her will to slip away... and that his eyes and his voice, was all she was aware of...that's all she wanted... that... and Paul.....

Something had happened to Paul.

This was awful. What the hell was he about to discover?

Outwardly, he remained calm and composed. He had to.

"Paul," he spoke and said nothing more.

She gasped. "You know. How could you possibly know?"

"Just let me touch your hand... just for a moment…" His voice took control though his mind raced. She acquiesced.

She withdrew her hand, hidden in the folds of the coat and smiled ruefully. "This coat… it was his…."

She raised her hand; he held it, just for a fleeting moment, and then let it fall away again.

"Ah yes..." he continued as he turned his face away and stared over towards one of the corners of the forgotten, invisible hall.

"Mmm... Yes... He passed over very suddenly didn't he?"

A lump formed in her throat, tears began to flow; she sniffled.

He smiled with kindness, his professionalism remaining in control. "It's OK, he's come here now, and he…"

Something he could not define disturbed him. This wasn't right. His smile dropped and he glanced, first in one direction, then another. His tenuous grip on the situation snapped, and his teetering confidence deserted him as his voice trailed off.

"There's so many here, so many voices that..."

He paused.

"That smell, the fragrance, it's so sweet and so pungent...does that mean anything?"

She looked puzzled and confused, and shook her head.

He stood abruptly and the scrape of the chair against the floor made her start.

"I'm sorry," he announced. "It isn't working, I think I'm overtired or something. It's not your fault."

Instinctively she stood as well. Feeling awkward and embarrassed, she fumbled for the buttons of her overcoat and looked down at the floor again as she did so.

"I must go," she said, and with that made a beeline for the door, almost stumbling on the way.

The door slammed behind her as a gust of wind howled through the hall, and it jarred him. After a second's hesitation, he ran after her but it was too late. As he stepped into the cold rain and night, he caught a glimpse of her in that overcoat as she disappeared into the darkness of the market square. But, once again, the features on her face were indistinguishable, she was too far distant. But, for a second, when another gust of wind made the rain and an autumn leaf hit her full in the face, he saw her flinch. He almost felt its sting on his own cheek.

The door banged shut behind him and caused him to jump, but when he turned towards her again, she had vanished into the night.

Deep down he'd hoped he'd meet her again, but not like this.

7

The following morning Sam resolved to put his unexpected encounter with Emma behind him, even though, if he was honest, he couldn't stop thinking about her. It was her face – hidden as it was under her collar behind a veil of sorrow. He had failed her, but in spite of his weariness of the halls and theatres, and the never-ending rows of expectant faces putting all that blind faith in him, the mystery surrounding her enticed and excited him.

But it wasn't just Emma though, it was the shock of Paul Carter's demise – the man with the towering stature and the brusque humour that wouldn't suffer fools gladly, but which Sam grudgingly admired – well it didn't seem possible; he seemed indestructible.

Nevertheless, a day off and sightseeing was the order of the day, with a visit to the nearby Roman army museum and library, which was a short distance away from Wraxbridge. History was his great passion, and with a wry smile, he thought how his friends teased him so, "Trust you!" they would say, "when you take a day off from dead people – there you are – locked away in their past."

Hardly anyone knew of the museum's existence, and he was not disappointed to find that he had the place to himself – perfect. He was free to wander from room to room and soak up the atmosphere and the ambience emanating from the ancient artefacts - carved stones, pillars, altars, gravestones, upon which weather-worn figures and icons, their faces with hollow eyes and gaping mouths, screamed out to him in silence. Figures and phantoms from long ago, far down the astral void and too far back in time for them to touch him – or so he thought.

But as he meandered from one display cabinet to the next and took in the artefacts – coins, jewellery, brooches, simeon ware, and even fragments of clothing – he sensed their long dead owners' hands touching them and owning them; he heard their breaths, sighs and whispers all around him. He didn't feel afraid or that he was intruding, but they resided there in the fluorescent-lit room with its dusty old glass cases, just as much as he did.

It was the sense of the ordinariness of the souls that surrounded him that left him spellbound; here, along the great frontier now known as Hadrian's Wall, a whole community had once thrived, not just the soldiers garrisoned around the military zone that the Wall formed, but the bustling town and community that grew around them; civilians, merchants, shop owners, inn keepers and traders, along with the wealthy and the humble, all going about their day to day lives. He felt no sense of oppression at all, but it was as real as he was. His thoughts turned to the fragments of parchment preserved out of the soil from the site nearby, their scribblings and day-to-day dramas and conversation frozen for all time.

He sat at the nearby desk and thumbed through the pages of a large and cumbersome tome that was on display. It was a typed transcript of the parchments and letters, and ran to several pages.

One letter, perhaps from an officer, or merchant, wished his friends well, and went on to say how pleased he was that their eldest son had at last settled down to some serious study. Another complained that their mother suffered from the ague, how expensive beer was now that there was a shortage, and that the fish from the stall holder in the market square was off, which was probably the cause for the stomach pains. One, probably from the Commanding Officer, described how he was looking forward to a few days leave at a friend's villa down south, where it was warmer.

For Sam, time was an illusion, so all this was happening in parallel to his own life.

But there was one section that held his attention in particular. It appeared to be a fragment of a diary, and was labelled by the librarians as: 'An account written by a young trainee archivist named Arrian, and who, as far as we can determine, was in the employ of the local governor, and attachÈ to the military.'

It read:

"I have just witnessed the most awful and traumatic night of my life; that and an act of betrayal. I could just about cope

and understand the need to crush and eradicate the barbaric rituals that took place on this night, but as to the horrific actions that ensued after the arrival of the soldiers - my Roman masters - that is all too much for me.

"I had first encountered the circle of stones a few seasons ago, and as archivist for the Governor of the province, I had accompanied the auxiliary units of the Legions when they first went on patrol, out into the expanse of the flatlands - the place where the stones lay. My instructions were to record and to draw images of the megaliths, and to try and gain some kind of understanding as to their purpose and relationship, if any, to the barbarian tribes and the deities they followed."

A thought shot abruptly into Sam's head, and he looked away to the far wall of the room, awe struck: A circle of stone? It had to be the same one. More threads of his encounters last summer were returning to him. With a sense of urgency, he read on:

"It was different then of course, when we first discovered the circle of stone, for then, when things had at last quietened down, and the Roman newcomers had subjugated the local tribesmen, the officers and auxiliaries of the garrison visited the circle purely as an idle curiosity. As life became better and safer, the merchants and tradesmen, and the civilians that had settled in the newly formed town around the garrison on the Great Wall, soon followed suit – it was after all, an attraction to any traveller. But no one knew of their purpose, not even the local Celtic tribes. All they could tell them was that they were very old – going back to the dark time, before the tribes of the land were formed. As to their purpose – this was lost in the aeons of time.

"This is where I came in – Lucius Arrian (to use my adopted Roman name) archivist and historian to the local Governor. It was my job to gain the confidence, and so infiltrate the local tribesmen and their elders. These were my father's kinsfolk (though I come from the south) but now I have adopted the Roman way – the modern way. The Roman occupiers knew that the rings of stone were scattered all over the lands nearby. The Great Wall, built on the direct orders of the noble Emperor Hadrian himself, had only just been completed. But the circles south of the Great Wall within the 'protection' of the Empire were the ones that caused concern for our new masters.

"They also knew that an elite performed certain religious practices at one such circle –a secretive sect, by priests who called themselves 'The Keepers of Knowledge' or as the locals nicknamed them, the Druids. That was fine; the Governor, like his peers throughout the Empire, could tolerate that, so long as it did not threaten the politics of the region. As the Governor told us: 'One should respect the deities of a foreign land when one wished to dwell there, and besides, it might even keep the barbarians docile and indifferent to Roman hegemony. However, to allow such secretive rituals to take place so close by, might cause a political destabilisation of the area, and that would not be tolerated.'

"As I drew and recorded the stones I soon became impressed and then overawed by their majesty. They form a near perfect circle, some three hundred and sixty five paces in diameter. They are set in a wide-open valley of heath and poor arable land, some distance from the garrison and adjacent *civilian settlement, and are approached along a gently rising slope of about a mile or so. However, a visitor would be unaware of the stones existence until he reached the top of the escarpment. There, the stones take you completely by surprise, waiting as they do below in the valley in their silent magnificence.*

"Beyond the stone circle, lay a row of three hills receding towards the distant horizon. And beyond there is the sea, and the great unknown – the very edge of Empire.

"On my first visit, an ancient oak grew at the centre; its mighty boughs gestured towards the sky like outstretched arms. The circle is unbroken all around, and huge blocks of megaliths mark an entrance, both at the east and west points. To the east, where one approached, two huge megaliths twice the size of a Centurion, formed the portal – the main gateway to the ring.

"One clear day, I spotted a tribal settlement nestling on the nearest of the hills consisting of round houses and fenced enclosures. The plumes of smoke gave its presence away from the thatched roofs as they billowed into the air. It was there that I befriended and gained the trust of a local priest known as Cernunnos, a 'Keeper of Knowledge' as he called himself. His tall stature and cruel dark eyes studied and judged you and betrayed intelligence far greater than that of a primitive priest.

"One winter's night amidst the archaic ritual of feasting in the open air before the glow and warmth of many fires – what strange customs the primitives seem to hang on to – Cernunnos, in his drunken reverie, spoke of the knowledge he

had acquired from his ancestors by word of mouth. Nothing had ever been recorded or written down. He boasted about his knowledge of the ceremonies that were performed two thousand years before him, and how the stones formed a magic container, which stored the wisdom and knowledge of generations of dead ancestors. As he continued to babble, he explained that through the pain and anguish of human sacrifice, this life force could be maintained, strengthened, and harnessed for his tribe's rebirth.

"He told me how the circle of stones came to be built. He explained that during the ancient and dark times, the priests from the clan who lived in the nearby lands visited this once sacred burial site with the close of every cycle of the moon in order to commune with the dead. They had cleared the circle of ground, and felled an ancient oak at its centre. From its wood, they had constructed the Charnel House on the place where it had grown. Here, the lifeless body of the Clan chief, the one named Mintaka, was lain, along with the two wives Alnilam and Alnitak, who had produced his offspring. It had been a terrible year for disease and famine.

"Once inside the walls of the hut, their skulls were removed, and their bodies were stretched out and exposed to the open air; to the wind, the rain and the sun – and to the vultures and scavengers – for only when their flesh had rotted away and their bones picked clean, would their souls be free to travel to the three sacred hills on the horizon – the place where the living dare not journey. Once there, they would enter the ground – the underworld – to dwell and preside over their descendants – and so determine the fate of the Clan.

"The seasons, then the years, wore on. The wooden walls of the Charnel House eroded and rotted away; the skeletons and bones became brittle and dry. The priests would use the skulls and the long bones for their rituals and ceremonies. But as the seasons and the years passed by, so did the priests and the clans' offspring. They died too, and their bodies were brought to the site by their offspring and placed with the others. The cycle was repeated by their descendents, and so to with each successive generation.

"A barrow of earth and stone was constructed around the disarray of bones from the dead. This would become the entrance to the underworld, the place where their spirits dwelled – the place where the priests, or the Keepers of Knowledge as they became known, would converse with their dead ancestors, and so seek guidance and wisdom.

"But despite the hardships caused by the cruelties of the cold, the crops failing, the hunger and the disease, and their infants dying, as the ages progressed, the people prevailed. And during the better times, the clans' population grew, as did other groups from all around. Eventually they all came to this sacred place to worship, and to inter their dead. But the secret power that arose from the concentration of the increasing number of dead ancestors became more difficult for the Keepers to handle, and so the time came when they brought the stones down from the sacred hills. They placed them so that they formed a sacred ring around the barrow. This circle of magic as they called it would confine the power of the spirits to this temple of worship – this holy site that contained the knowledge of the dead. This concentration of power within so

small an area inside the ring would allow the Keepers to tap into this source of knowledge.

"This ritual within the sacred circle of magic became the custom for generations. On one day of each year, the coldest and darkest day, when the Keepers knew that the golden orb within the sky shone pale yellow and feeble in the watery grey sky for only a short length of time, and when the earth was hard, cold and damp, and the trees were dead, the people would come to the circle in their droves. The priests would chant and parade with their skulls and bones of the long since dead, as the people passed by them with their funerary urns on their pilgrimage to the stones. The urns, containing the burnt ashes of their dead – the brothers, sisters, wives and infants that had perished during the passing of the year – were offered and interred underneath the stones.

"They knew that their remains would rot and return to the earth, just like the plants and beasts that shared their world, but their spirits and thoughts - their consciousness – would be absorbed into the stones, which were hard, permanent and enduring.

"Then the feasting and the merriment would begin, and as the intoxicating potions and smoke took hold, the dead would rise – for that night only.

"This was the beginning of the re-birth. The flesh had been returned to the earth to make it fertile again. In the days to come, the golden orb in the sky would become warmer and stronger, and the woods and forests would reawaken with life. The crops would grow, and the women be impregnated – some on that very night of feasting. Everything that had died had

been returned to the sacred earth, so as to start the process of re-birth. Such was the way of things.

"Then, as Cernunnos staggered to his feet and stumbled over to a large oak chest, he withdrew a skull and long bone. They appeared all yellow, gnarled and cracked and he thrust them towards my face. He claimed they belonged to his earliest ancestors. Still intoxicated, he demanded that we visit the ring of stone that very night. The cold crisp air did not appeal, but judging by his demeanour, I thought it best to acquiesce.

"As we staggered and shivered down the open hill, away from the warmth and glow of the campfire, and out into the starry darkness, Cernunnos continued with his mutterings and incomprehensible blether about events that were supposed to have taken place two thousand years before us. We entered the circle, and with the skull clasped in his hand like a mitre, he held the long bone aloft and pointed to a row of three stars rising in the east.

"I looked up and beheld an awe-inspiring vision, as the constellation we know as Orion (not that Cernunnos would know it as that) rose from behind the blackened shape of the hills on the horizon. Orion, the Greek hunter, was once again starting its journey across the night sky, and as always its sheer size and majesty filled me with wonder. He was referring to the stars that formed the belt around Orion's girth.

"Cernunnos continued with his excited chatter and told me that the hills were where their Gods dwelt, and that next year, when the alignment was perfect, then his peoples' time will have come! He pointed to a few of the stones as he walked erratically up and down from one to another, and then his excitement

ceased and he became serious and more lucid again. My unease increased when he next spoke:

'Sacrifices... we have to appease and surrender to our ancestors that which is precious to us, if they are to help us.'

"With trepidation in my heart, I moved towards the nearest megalith and peered into the darkness on the ground. The starlight had cast a dark black shape at the mound of the base, and I knew that I was looking at a pile of disturbed earth. As my eyes grew accustomed, with a cry I recoiled, as I recognised what I was looking at: a pile of burnt black ashes lay before me, with a trinket or maybe a bronze ring, together with a white skull shining smooth and pale in the light neatly placed at the centre. The skull appeared to be staring up at me in a truly pitiful way.

"Something touched my shoulder, making me jump out of my wits. The long bone pressed down on me, and as I stood up, and turned around, the dark eyes of Cernunnos bore into me. He said: 'Five more offerings my friend, five more... pure youth... virgins, untouched and unsullied. This is the price we have to pay... our youth… our future. We return their pureness and their fertility to the ground where our ancestors lay... in return for their blessing.'"

By the time Sam started out on the return to Wraxbridge, night had fallen. He sped along the highway known as the great military road that skirted along the south side of Hadrian's Wall. But his thoughts meandered from the writings of Arrian, which re-played over and over as though it was in the present, and actually a personal letter to him, rather than a fragment of an event occurring two thousand years ago, and then to that of Paul Carter. He saw Carter in his mind's eye, wielding the hammer as the false wall in Edwulf's tower collapsed and the look of triumph on the big man's face that followed. Then the mentioning by Arrian of the bronze ring hit him, and to the one on the murdered girl, and those found on the skeletal remains that keep occurring.

With a rude awakening, a loud scrape by a protruding branch on the side of the car shook Sam from his daydreaming. With a jerk of the wrist, he corrected the course of the speeding car back to safety. He blinked his eyes back to alertness - he was more tired than he thought. It was a clear night but the road, though broad and well surfaced, was deceptively winding, and the dips and rises made it easy for him to lose control of his speed. The headlights shone brightly on the cats' eyes, and on the dense row of trees lunging at him grotesquely on either side of the road as he steered around each approaching bend. A flurry of leaves came tumbling down from a bough overhead, caught in the autumn breeze, and their reflections in the car headlights shone like a swarm of luminous moths. His eyes were heavy. The weather was turning, and he thought what a cold and windswept land this must be, now that the summer visitors had returned to their other lives. A tell tale spray of rain hit the windscreen, as if to confirm his last thought.

The road seemed to twist for mile after mile, with more hills, dips, and the never-ending rows of trees. His tiredness increased. The rain became heavy, as did the wind, which lashed the spray against the windscreen. He peered into the darkness ahead, and hunched his shoulders and arms around the steering wheel as his progress slowed.

He switched on the car radio. Perhaps a little music or late night chat might make him feel a little less alone.

Just then a tiny speck of light, like a star on the horizon, flickered into view. After a moment or two, he realised that the headlamps had caught a tiny distant road sign in their beam. He smiled to himself with relief, for he knew that once passed this tiny beacon, the road would even out onto open moorland, and a stretch of good roadway. He would soon be back in Wraxbridge.

The road straightened out into the distance as he began his descent into the open low lying terrain; each cats eye waiting it's turn to light up, and show him the way.

All seemed well again but the sudden popping noise from the radio, followed by a hissing crackle, then silence, soon put paid to that. He looked down at the dials in search of an answer and then looked up again into the distance. An involuntary spasm of pins and needles shot down his spine; he could see figures moving in the distance, caught in the headlights. He placed his foot on the brakes and the car slowed, even though they were some way off – just before the road dipped and the land rose again. As the car slowed to an amble, his fear turned to puzzlement; they didn't seem aware of his approach. There were three or four of them, and the beam of his lights caused flashes of silver and white to spark off their bodies, as though they were clad in metal or some such material. How odd! Had they broken down? He could not see where their vehicle was.

He was getting quite close now. He tried to reassure himself by assuming that they would move from the road as he approached and allow him to pass. He would just drive on; that would be best he thought, but his mouth became dry with fearful anticipation.

But his fear turned to alarm as two of the figures turned and headed straight for him, and so by the time he hit the brakes hard it was too late. The car skidded and protested against the wetness and downward sloping gradient of the road.

"I'm gonna hit you," he whimpered uselessly to himself.

Then it all happened so quickly.

An ashen, featureless face, now almost on top of the bonnet, loomed out of the murk. Instinctively, he spun the steering wheel. He expected to hear the inevitable sickening thud...

Instead, the car screeched and spun, making him hit his head on something; he wasn't sure whether he was upside down or the right way up. There was a terrific thumping in his head, and then he realised that his face was pressed against the side window, with the steering wheel and column crushing his body. The car lights shone into the night sky, lighting up the rain as it blew aimlessly in every direction by the breeze.

But, save for the wind, all was silent; there was no sound from the car. It had stalled, and he was in the ditch.

When he tried to move, an acute pain overcame him. He was stuck – paralysed almost. His fevered brain detected a movement outside and his encroaching terror closed in on him still further. Whoever, or whatever it was, he hoped it would be over very quickly.

A figure, dressed in armour he guessed, stood outside and watched him. He couldn't make out its face, and a mist began to envelope him as he fought against his encroaching unconsciousness. It approached and pressed its face upon the glass – next to his. Sam's laboured breathing increased as his panic welled up within him, but then he realised that the silent watcher breathed too, in unison with his own. He was struggling to keep his reason – maybe the thing on the other side was his own reflection – yes – maybe.

Feeling light-headed, he stepped away from the overturned car, surprisingly with little effort.

He was outside now. He turned around, and to the circle of stone. He recognised the three soldiers he was with – of course they were his comrades. He knew he was inside the body of Arrian because the voice in his head told him so. He was living through Arrian and replaying his memory….

He sat cross-legged within the circle adjacent to one of the smaller weathered stones. The pit, at the stone's base, was open again, and exposed the burnt ash and bronze ring. Five torches placed between the megaliths burned brightly, and shone like red malevolent eyes in the night. He was an honoured guest of Cernunnos but his heart was heavy, he knew that his betrayal of his maverick friend was imminent.

Once again, the air was cold and crisp and the moon, as it rose, bathed the ground with a pale luminescent light. The stones appeared ghostly, almost animated as the light reflected from their weathered sandstone surface. Cernunnos, now dressed in his priests robes and clasping the skull and long-bone, appeared buoyant as he flitted from stone to stone, then back to the huge oak tree at the centre. A mask, out of which protruded the antlers of some long dead beast, hid his face. Two others, dressed similarly and behaving in the same way, accompanied him. Occasionally they would stop and gaze skyward as they anxiously waited for the last remaining wisps of clouds to disappear.

Arrian's attention was drawn to a group of men who had been piling bracken against the oak, no doubt with the intention of starting a fire. Now they had abandoned their task and were leaving the spot in order to assist the arrival of a small precession from the opposite entrance. As soon as the tightly packed group of figures began to disperse, a terrible sense of dread began to fill Arrian. There, at the centre of the group, a row of five young females, naked and pale in the moonlight, stood as if in a trance, chained and manacled. Then, one by one, they were released by their captors, and frog-marched over to the standing stones on the far side. Once there, they were lashed and bound to the stones and more bracken was pressed at their feet. The victims offered no resistance, and remained trance-like and torpid. Their task over, the captors returned to the centre.

Arrian winced; time was running out.

Cernunnos gestured towards the night-sky with the long bone and shouted excitedly:

"In the names of Mintaka, Alnilam, and Alnitak, I make these offerings."

The row of three stars had appeared over the horizon, and was rising over the hills in perfect alignment. With a grand gesture, he pointed the bone in the direction of the oak. Using the torches, the men started the fire. As the smouldering turned to a red glow, the fire came to life. One man took a torch and crossed to a stone where a victim was bound. He lit the bracken beneath her feet. As the flames grew and flickered, for the first time she began to flinch and twitch; the heat from the flames were causing her drug-induced hypnosis to wear off. But, before he could take this awful moment in, the man drew a long sword from his robe, and with a lightening quick stroke, severed the head with a single blow.

Arrian felt the bile from his stomach rise within him.

A second man lit a torch from the fire around the oak and then walked to another stone, where another helpless victim was bound, and repeated the process. He felt sure he could hear the cries and moans of another of the females; she was waking before her time was due. Where the hell were the soldiers? He began to weep; it was just too horrible to bear. What reasoning, what evil could provoke anyone to perform such acts of sacrifice? His

Roman masters had told him of such lurid practices taking place on this windswept northern island, laying on the northern fringes of the Empire – forsaken by the gods – well now he knew it to be true. He also knew that such ritual acts of sacrifice took place with his own people, but that was only with animals, domesticated livestock, or even prisoners of war in extreme cases. He recognised the need for pain; giving up something that was valuable, even revered in order to show the gods that you would make these sacrifices in return for their blessing and protection. But to take it to this level – to sacrifice the flower of the people's youth – the fertile birth givers of the tribes' future generations was just unimaginable.

The flames around the oak had taken hold. The heat and smoke had replaced the cool opaque light with that of a fiery orange-red glow. As Arrian's nerve cracked, he wept uncontrollably.

The priests stood before the fire, and as the charred remains of the bark splintered and fell to the earth, the blackened outlines of three headless skeletons standing in a row appeared amongst the flames where the oak had stood. Oblivious to the spitting fire and falling embers, each priest in turn took the ancient skull that they carried and placed it on top of each skeletal torso. Then, from the corner of his eye, Arrian witnessed the second female's decapitation.

He cursed the auxiliary troops delay in arriving and began to doubt they were ever coming, but then, as if in answer to his prayer, a different noise more familiar to him caught his attention. From the opposite entrance – from the direction he knew to be that of the fort encampment – the soldiers arrived.

The clanking of the armour, and the shiny red glow of its metal from the fires, came like a beacon of reason to Arrian.

He stood euphoric and prepared to welcome the Centurion, until he realised that the Commanding Officer himself led the incursion. This was a rare occurrence indeed; this wasn't the plan. The officer barked the order "free for all", and the troops rapidly broke rank. The horror was not over.

The first of the druids fell bloody, broken and lifeless on the ground as soon as the auxiliaries charged into them. In a panic, the tribesmen began to flee in all directions but with a sickening ease, the troops cut them all down with a short stabbing movement into the belly with their swords. The second priest, as he tottered and backed away from an advancing soldier, toppled into the flames, the ferocity of which rapidly consumed him. In a matter of moments, the screams and cries from the worshippers fell silent, as the lifeless heaps of their bodies scattered the ground.

Arrian's brief euphoria had evaporated, and as the Commanding Officer marched purposely over to him, his harsh face and cold eyes bore into him.

"Lucius Arrian! No-one is to remain alive here by the direct orders of the Governor."

He knew then that even the hapless victims were to be despatched. His look of utter despair prompted the Commander to speak more:

"For the honour of our Legion, we will stamp out these vile activities with utter ruthlessness – let it be an example to those who dare to challenge the authority of our august and deified Emperor Hadrian."

The soldiers stood by the stones expectant, with their swords still drawn. With a single nod from the Commander, they promptly thrust them into the bellies of the surviving victims, still strapped helplessly to the stones.

One solitary remaining figure emerged from behind the fire, shouting and cursing as he did so. His mask had fallen, and he recognised him as Cernunnos. A soldier dragged him in front of his comrades, and he sank to his knees He cowered before them, his eyes rolling and delirious.

"No matter, no matter," he babbled. "You have finished the job. All the virgins have been sacrificed, and their blood has been returned... it... it has soaked into the earth of our ancestors and the ground will be fertile again. I shall return once more, in two thousand years, when I…"

But he was cut short as the soldiers raised their swords and chopped Cernunnos to pieces.

For a moment an eerie silence prevailed, save for the cracking and splintering of the wood as it burned. But Cernunnos was wrong; the sacrifice had not been completed. Although he was not certain, Arrian thought he saw the naked form of a female with long, and plaited hair worn in ringlets. Silhouetted against the orange-red light of the fire, he watched her flee from the dreadful scene. She appeared from behind, or perhaps from within one of the stones, and then swiftly and silently disappeared again into the darkness, unseen by the melee of soldiers clustered within the bloody arena.

But then, he could not really be sure of what his eyes were telling him. Raindrops were hitting him in the face, and yet he could not feel them – they neither stung nor soaked him. An ice-cold sheet seemed to press into his face. Glass – he was still trapped in the car after all. The figure, now clad in shiny yellow, loomed over him as it shone an intense white light into his eyes. It blinded him.

The car door opened and he lurched forward.

8

"It's really good of you to take me in like this Emma, I feel like some kind of a stray."

"You make it sound as if I should offer you a saucer of milk."

He noticed the momentary smile on her lips, and how she raised those long and graceful eyelashes in order to study him with her pale blue eyes – but only for a moment, then she lowered them again and the sorrowful look on her face returned. She wore her fair hair long and straight - a little untidy he thought, so that her downward glance made it cascade and hide her face. But there was a hidden and serene beauty about that face which he felt sure would return, once the grieving was over.

They were sitting at the opposite sides of a small table in her kitchen. He sensed that she was unsure about her unexpected visitor. She didn't know what to make of him. Nevertheless he found himself relating his psychic experiences from the previous night to her. When he came to, an ambulance man dressed in yellow oilskins had pulled him from the stricken car. Apparently, he was delirious, and the only words he muttered that were comprehensible were 'Great Stones', 'megaliths' and 'Emma'. Later, the nurse on the ward put two and two together and concluded that he must have connections with the recent archaeological dig in the area, for she knew that Emma was the widow of a man recently killed there after a tragic accident. In desperation she telephoned her, and persuaded her to visit him. As soon as she realised it was Sam, she agreed to care for him – just for a day or two.

"You are the only person I know here in Wraxbridge. I'm so far from home," he tailed off.

"No… no, really it's alright." Her eyes rose to meet his again, and this time her glance was slower to fall away. "You were kind to me the other day, even though our meeting was so brief. I want to return that kindness…you can stay here in my flat if you like…for a day or two."

"But you don't know me."

"I know *about* you… and your reputation. Besides, looking at the state of you, you're hardly in a position to do anything improper."

Sam leant back from the table and sighed as he fingered the dressing on his forehead. His head ached and the bruises on his arm made it feel all stiff and sore.

"That's very good of you. My car has been towed to that small garage in the centre of the village. Apparently it's in better shape than I am, so it will be ready when I go home."

"Go home? What will you do?"

"I'll return to my hotel when I feel better, then head south for home. There's not much else I can do."

"Stay!" she cried with a sudden plea. "Stay for a while."

The sudden urgency in her voice surprised him, as did her placing her hand across the table onto his.

"Perhaps… if you could give me another sitting… I promise it will be the last."

Self-consciously she withdrew her hand and looked down at the table once more.

"Besides, wouldn't you like to find out more about your Roman soldier?"

He thought to himself for a moment. He was supposed to be taking time off from all of this, but there were too many coincidences here: first Emma arrives back in his life, and then when he spoke with her in the village hall there was that sweet and sickly fragrance that overpowered him. He remembered that from long ago, when he was an infant during those terrible dreams – phantoms that had returned from his childhood. Why all of this now? Then there were the megaliths.

Eventually he nodded, then stood from the chair. He drew the curtains in the tiny kitchen window, and then walked down the steps into the sitting room part of the flat. Her living quarters seemed so small and sparse. He closed the door of her bedroom, which led off from another short flight of steps so as to shut them in, and drew the remaining curtains. He pulled the two armchairs together so that they faced each other.

"The darker and more ambient it is, the better," he explained. "Do you have any candles?"

She reached for a couple from the cupboard under the sink and handed them to him. He lit them, and placed them by the glass-fronted cabinet case next to the armchairs. He stared into the cabinet for a moment as the candlelight reflected on all the ornaments and artefacts with a soft orange-yellow glow. There were brooches, silverware, coins and tiny pieces of pottery, some broken, some intact all giving off an aura of great age - relics and finds from times distant. Next to the cabinet, a bookshelf was filled with dog-eared books and catalogues of finds.

"Well, I *am* an archaeologist!" She was watching him.

"You're a collector of objects and thoughts from the past, not unlike myself," he smiled to her.

He gestured for her to sit opposite him, and as she did so, she looked into his eyes and brushed away the hair from her face, which had helped to hide her away.

The room was so small and the candlelight so warming, that, with the long shadows they cast over the nearby bookcase and surroundings, the room became very intimate. Their faces were but a few feet apart. Without questioning, she put out her hand, and allowed him to hold it again, just for a brief moment, before it slipped away.

"Paul," he said quite simply.

But this time he didn't look away - his gaze fixed into her eyes. He was sure he felt her sigh, and her heart miss a beat the moment he spoke the name. He had done this so many times before, but in spite of himself, he felt a special sorrow for this lady in front of him. Not wise to become involved, he thought, but he couldn't help himself.

The now familiar, sad and tearful smile appeared before him.

"Mm… yes," he looked away into the darkness, and sensed Paul's presence. An image of his face shone opaquely in the shadows, visible only to him silent though serene. And then Sam looked back towards Emma again.

"He passed to the other side very quickly, didn't he?"

"Yes."

"Something's falling... he's on the ground... on top of him."

"Yes."

"But, you know... he's smiling, and he's saying to you that he's OK now... really... there's no pain, not then... not now…"

Her rueful smile broadened as the tears flowed.

"But I wasn't there for him when it happened, and I just want... just want to say I love him, and ... to say goodbye, just one last time... there's so much I never said."

"It's OK ... OK... yes," he continued to turn away to the darkness, and back to her again. "He's smiling; he says that he loves you too, but that you must move on, you must..." He paused, " I'm seeing a small object, a black disc, or a plate maybe?"

She shook her head.

"Two people joined?" he ventured.

"Oh... oh the medallion," she looked over to the bookcase, and to the small objects inside cast in shadow by the candlelight, and hidden by the gloom.

"The Betrothal Medallion…"

"Yes... yes... he's saying, look at it, keep it always, and think of us... yes... but move on..."

She gasped again, and she felt a sense of release as the tension flowed away. He was here. Paul was really here, in this very room.

Sam continued his silent conversation with the unseen soul, nodding and smiling and muttering to himself, until finally he sensed Paul's spirit had become restless, driven by a yearning to move on and away. After a deep sigh he turned to her, "It's time to go."

She nodded in acquiescence, and with that he arose. He snuffed out the candles one by one, and turned on the table lamp.

They sat there in silence for a few moments.

"Feel better?"

"A little," she said, drying her eyes.

"So when did this happen?"

"Last month, during the storms. After more arguments with Forrester, he'd agreed to have him back on site. Forrester had to if he wanted me to remain at the dig. Paul and I came as a package, that as we *came*… Anyway, Paul had started another archaeological dig, this time just north of the town, near the Wall, and not entirely with Mr Forrester's approval. Typical Paul – gung ho! Shoot first and answer questions after."

Amidst the tears, they both laughed at the thought of Paul going forth, and letting no-one, not even Forrester get in his way.

She continued, "It was an amazing site. We were in the middle of excavating a whole wall of a Mile castle – you know they call them that; it's a kind of lookout post you see, with smaller turrets placed regularly, one Roman mile along the Wall. A military temple had been excavated nearby to where we were."

She smiled to herself as she reflected on what she said.

"I've always worked with Paul. We met when we were students, and we made a great team."

He smiled. "I remember you telling me when we first spoke in your car. It seems so long ago now."

"It's me who gets to record and catalogue any of the finds…the actual archaeology, that's his… or rather *was* his field." She checked herself again.

Then she leaned forward and looked into Sam's eyes closely, "Sam, I've never told anyone this before…"

She hesitated and Sam's heart leapt. She was about to confide in him, open her heart – something he could only wish for last summer.

"But I had a bad feeling about all of this, ever since the body of the girl was found over at the stone circle, though Paul dismissed it all as nerves. I guess that's why I left you that rather cryptic note; I was looking for some one to confide in. And you know Paul had become increasingly strained and withdrawn. I never really knew what Forrester was looking for either.

"Anyway, Paul had let his enthusiasm get the better of him as usual, and he had scrambled into a trench near the newly excavated wall, before the mechanical digger had fully moved away. All of a sudden, after a gust of wind, the whole earth, along with most of the excavation, collapsed before he could get clear. OK, so I know he took a bit of a cavalier attitude to his work, but he was always careful and articulate - you know that - and he always had a scientific approach. And remember Forrester just didn't want him there after once he'd found out what he wanted to know about the megaliths...about the sacrificial rituals. By then, he was taking more of an interest in me...Paul didn't like that."

She closed her eyes, and shook her head, and became silent for a moment. Then, after a gulp, she appeared to be composed again, and continued: "And you see I wasn't there when it happened. I never got a chance to say goodbye."

She choked back a tear and her voiced failed her again. He put his hand on hers, and then - he couldn't help himself - he moved it so that it rested it under her chin, so that their eyes met again...so close.

"I know it's irrational and all that...I'm supposed to be a scientist, but..." She suddenly laughed amidst the tears, and it caused her hand to fall away from his and so the intimacy was broken, "but thank you...thank you."

He continued to study her - the expressions on her

face and the movement of her body on the chair. She was calmer now.

"The enquiries and all the paperwork seem to have been going on for ever, but as soon as it is over with, I shall leave. I have no one either you know. None of the team has the will to continue with the dig anyway…it just seems cursed, so it's been abandoned."

She looked up and frowned.

"But the Betrothal Medallion, how could you possibly know about that?"

He shrugged. "May I see it?"

She reached over, and with an arm outstretched, so close to him now, opened the glass door of the bookcase and pulled out a small object from the dark recess. But as she did so, the sight and invisible scent of her body, and the gentle rustling sound of her blouse against the curve of her bosom as it tapered to her slim waist, affected him. Such delicate feminine grace; it was a far cry from his first impression; that of a woman physically small and of plain features, hidden by long and lank hair, and shrouded in an overcoat. And when she opened out the palm of her hand to reveal the black medallion, the size of an old penny, the delicate gracefulness of that hand touched him.

He took the medallion and held it to the light.

"It's beautiful isn't it?" she said. "It's made of Whitby jet. Very rare."

The carving upon it depicted a man and a woman facing each other. They had large eyes, and their mouths were open as though their lips were about to embrace in a kiss. It was obviously taken from a classical Roman sculpture, but beautifully carved and amazingly preserved, even down to such detail as the man's noble beard, and the woman's hair, worn up in classical style, to reveal her slender neck and naked shoulder.

"It's known as a Betrothal Medallion. Paul and I fell in love with it and… well I know it's wrong and we broke a sacred rule of archaeology, but we didn't record the find. Instead, we kept it for ourselves. Don't judge us."

He smiled. It was just like his adventure with Paul and the discovery of the bronze ring.

"Why should I judge you? It's very beautiful as you say, and a symbol of your love. You will treasure it."

She seemed quite relaxed now and walked over to the kitchen area to make coffee.

"We're out. I'm just nipping out to the shop for some supplies. I'll be back soon."

He sat there alone for a few moments in idle contemplation, gazing at the jet-black stone, made alive and vibrant by the lamplight. Then, all of a sudden the shock hit him. The smell... that sweet, seductive fragrance – it had returned, and it was all around him once again – so it couldn't be coming from Emma after all, because he would have noticed it earlier, and indeed, it would have alarmed him. No… it must be emanating from something associated with her… something she cherished. Abruptly his glare turned to the object in his hand, now tingling, and vibrating on his skin. There were voices too…voices attempting to break through from the other side. The spirits had returned. So that was it! The medallion – he had got it wrong, or at least partially so. Maybe it wasn't just for Emma's sake that Paul's spirit had contacted him. He had made him aware of the jet stone's existence; there was a link to it, and the sweet and intoxicating fragrance, which had haunted him from way back. And he thought of the Roman soldier too, his passive face staring at him through the windscreen, and now here – for he sensed that he was in this very room…so there *was* a link.

It was clear to him that spirits from the other side were trying to tell him, or perhaps show him something – but what?

The sound of the door latch told him of her return. She moved to the kitchen without turning her face to him and began preparing coffee. He sensed that something was wrong. She had become agitated again judging by her rapid, fidgety movements.

"Emma, what's wrong?"

She stopped as though the sound of his voice had frozen her still, but she remained with her back turned.

"Emma?"

She turned. The colour had drained from her face again and her brow was furrowed. She folded her arms and began to pace to and fro.

"There's one more thing I haven't told you… the dead girl… it's just possible that I may have known her… through Megan you see…"

"Ah Megan, I'd forgotten about her. You mentioned that name in the note you handed me when I first met you. But this is serious Emma..."

She steeled herself. "I only said it was possible. We knew of a young woman by the name of Fleur. She was a rebel, a waif and stray. I befriended her only because I felt sorry for her. But then she disappeared. She seemed very close to Megan who offered her work of some sort. Oh I suppose she's headed off for Newcastle or Edinburgh maybe, there was nothing for her here. It's just a coincidence." But as she spoke, there was no eye contact as she stared down at the floor. "Now then, coffee..."

More importantly though, he knew he had to persuade Emma to take him to the place where the amulet was found.

One thing he knew for sure. There was no way that he was going home now.

9

They spent the day together. It wasn't a conscious decision, it just happened. He'd dismissed all negative thoughts of Emma's innocence or otherwise over the dead girl. He was deeply attracted to the grieving widow – he couldn't forget that even if he wanted to.

They wandered around Wraxbridge and along the quaint, grey-bricked shopping mall and thoroughfares. With arms linked, they explored the cafes and shops, and finished with a stroll along the riverbank and the old bridge, with its sandstone colours shining golden in the autumn afternoon sunshine.

They paused for a moment on the opposite bank from where the town was situated, and next to the arch of the bridge.

"There was a Roman bridge here, but this one dates back to the seventeenth century," she had to explain.

It made him smile and he looked into her face as it shone in the sunlight. But then the despair came through again – just a hint from the sadness in her eyes and the down turned mouth. She shuddered as if the ozone and spray from the rushing water had caused a chill breeze to hit her and sharpen the pain. She looked over to the deserted beer garden on the opposite bank. He knew she was thinking of Paul.

"Everywhere is so empty now... no people anywhere," she sighed.

"All gone home... close season."

"Home... where's your home?" She linked arms with him, and gently pulled him so that they would begin a stroll along the river path.

"I live in the Midlands where I grew up."

"Your parents, or your wife, are they down there?"

"No...no, I'm quite alone. I never knew my father, and my mother left when I was quite small."

"That's awful!" She held onto his sleeve more tightly.

The path veered away from the river and towards a tunnel of overhanging trees, where the autumn sunlight barely had the strength to filter through.

"Oh, no but I was brought up in a happy and secure home by relatives. Really, it was just a normal childhood... well, except for the dreams. Of course, I wasn't to know that I was psychic. My mother just went one day... she just disappeared. Maybe she went to be with the man who used to visit her... a tall, frightening man in a dark coat. I think he had some sort of hold over her. I wouldn't have said they were lovers, but how was I to know? My aunt and uncle flatly refused to talk about it."

She turned to face him, with an inquisitive and yet sympathetic look in her eyes.

"But hey, listen to me," he was anxious to explain, "I'm really quite normal and functional! I was fed, clothed, and had a normal upbringing."

And he was keen to move on, "Careful, it's muddy underfoot, we should go into the open."

They continued on their way, until the path led them to the open and to the river again. They paused, and looked out onto the blue fast flow of the water as it babbled noisily and (it seemed) impatiently, as it collided with boulders, fallen branches and bracken that barred its way.

"The river swell's high today," she muttered.

"I love it here," was all that he wanted to say as he breathed in the refreshing air.

"Yes, it's my home, even though I've no-one now. Typical Paul! His finances were in a mess – he thought I'd deal with all that sort of thing. His personal secretary, that's what I was! But once his affairs are settled, I'll be left with the flat and nothing more, especially now that Mr Forrester's big fat pay cheque won't be forthcoming."

A faint call of shouting and excited voices drifted over the breeze from somewhere further down the bank. She turned her face towards the sound and squinted into the light, and then a broad grin formed on her lips.

"I know those voices, come, let's see."

She pulled at him again, and they had only walked a few paces when the winding embankment gave way to a broad and gravel-strewn bank. A group of youths lounged along the grassy edge, amidst empty beer cans. Tapes and ropes cordoned off the surroundings.

"Hard at work then?" she called to them as she

smiled. "These are the students from the uni' I have the dubious pleasure of working with. They're helping here with an archaeological dig," she explained to Sam.

"Alright Emm? It's our day off," they laughed as they called back to her.

"Nine a.m. then, tomorrow, sharp!" she mocked.

For a moment, her optimistic bonhomie came through; just like the Emma he had known when he first met her.

"See the remains of the abutments among the stones in the water? They formed the foundations of where the Roman bridge stood," she explained as she waved back at them, and then put her hand around his arm again.

"Friends?"

"Yes, I like their company, and they've taken my mind off things. But for how long can an ageing graduate like me keep hanging around with students? They'll soon be gone. Come on, we'd better be getting back. It's getting cold and the sun will go down soon."

"Getting back? Where are we going?"

"Back to my flat of course. I'll cook us a meal."

Sam looked dubiously at the broken remains of the stone bridge submerged in the crystal water, and then back at Emma.

"What's wrong?" she asked all concerned.

"Don't tell me… roast field mice marinated in honey, and heavily garnished in a sauce made from fish genitals… that's what the Romans ate isn't it?"

She playfully jabbed him in the ribs with her fist.

"It's fish giblets, not genitals, you wally! And no, it'll be beef curry."

"That'll do."

They laughed as they made their way back, just as the golden sunlight began to fade.

***

"Sam, I'd like you to stay around... at least for a while. I don't like being alone, now that Paul..."

She stared down at the half eaten food as she sat on the opposite side of the small kitchen table to him. He poured the last of the wine into her glass.

"I'll stay as long as you like." He never thought he would be uttering those words to her.

"Stay here tonight then." She looked up at him with a look of hope in her eyes. "You can sleep in the living room, it can be quite comfortable. It's too soon for anything more... you understand?"

It was more than he could have hoped for, and he was overwhelmed by the trust she was putting in him, and for once, *he* no longer felt alone.

And that night, as he shuffled uncomfortably from the floor to the armchairs, his only thought was not to betray that trust. But as his ears and senses grew accustomed to the wind and the patter of autumn rain on the windowpanes of the tiny flat, his mind grew tired and consciousness began to slip away...

Then he sensed it again... and so soon after the last

time… that all too familiar sweet smell of jasmine, now stronger than ever before. In his half waking and sleeping state it took a few moments to register, but a bright and dazzling orange light, which he recognised as sunlight, blazed through his eyelids. As he opened them, the warmth of the sun bathed his face. The smell of jasmine was strong, but for the first time he was not afraid, this time it tasted sweet and exciting, and a stirring grew within his loins, and butterflies formed in his stomach. He was young; he was aroused... a giggle echoed in his ears, and as he turned, a fresh and youthful face filled his sight. Sam, or at least what was left of the conscious part of Sam's will from inside him, recognised her.

"Arrian, you're naughty," the girl sighed, "you're dreaming again aren't you? About your soldier friends, about conquests... glory and far away lands."

They were both kneeling against a grassy mound, with hills and moorland far away behind them. He looked into the distance with wonder at the mighty Wall of stone, all new and complete as it snaked over the hills in both directions as far as the eye could see. It impressed him and yet filled him with awe. Nearby, the gentle trickling of a stream babbled away.

She giggled again and beamed playfully at him as the sun beat down on her face. She took his hand and clasped it to her breast, playfully rubbing it round and round with her own, with a wicked and coquettish glint in her eye. The freckles on her skin, which he had always teased her about in their childhood, were fading.

"I'm almost a woman now," she smiled contentedly, as if she was reading his mind. Then the smile faded, and she became quite serious.

"Oh Arrian marry me, like you said you would. You do still love me don't you?"

"Of course I do Brigit, you know that."

"Then why are you always talking about joining the army?"

"You know why. The officers like me. I impressed them with all my cataloguing and drawings of the great circle of stone, but now I want more excitement. My mother's kin come from the south. She says if I join now, I can learn skills, a trade maybe. I'll be well paid and fed, and when I leave, I can start my own business here. I can become a farrier, or own a shop, many shops... or I could buy a brew house... that would be fun, all that beer."

She pulled his hand away from her.

"No! You just want to fight, you think it's big."

"I can still marry you Brige."

"You know very well that's not true," her voice began to quiver, and a tear formed in her eye.

"You're not allowed to marry until you leave the army, and you're stuck in there for twenty five years!"

"Yes, yes, but everyone knows that the Commandants of nearly all the Legions turn a blind eye... they allow all their men to take mistresses and raise families. Why should this one be any different? Their unions become formalised when they retire, so it'll be alright Brige I promise…"

"No, it isn't all right." She stood abruptly and looked

down at him. "My father was quite clear; you heard what he said when you turned down his offer to allow you to work on his farmstead. He was quite hurt you know, he thought of you as the son he never had."

"He'll come round."

"No!" Her agitation grew. "Unless we marry, he has forbidden us to see each other again. He's quite determined."

"No Brige, you're lying."

She began to sob, and amidst the chokes she stuttered: "His very words were: 'our union could never be'... yes, he said 'this could never be'... and if I lose you, I'd much rather die here by this stream where we made our betrothal. I don't care when they say we're so young. I love you so much..."

And with that, she turned away and tossed a small, black, disc-like medallion onto the ground. She walked away from him with her cries and sobs gradually fading from his ears. His vision became blurred, and at the same time the rain and the wind of the night returned.

Now fully awake, Sam sat on the armchair and rubbed his eyes wearily as he sighed. Then he noticed the betrothal medallion still resting on the bookcase since the morning's sÈance. He thought of the soldier boy called Arrian, and that pungent smell of jasmine. Twice now his spirit had resided and breathed within him. Clearly the medallion would play a crucial part in laying his ghost to rest. At the same time he was aware of the steady and soft rhythmic breathing of a sound asleep Emma from the open door of the bedroom. He looked at the medallion again and realised what he had to do.

He walked over to the door and switched on the light.

She stirred and sat upright, as his sudden intrusion startled her. She gasped, and her brow furrowed before she became fully awake. Self consciously, she wrapped the duvet around her more tightly but it was not enough and her shoulder remained exposed. Her leg remained naked, too, and appeared sensual in the warm light. Her hair fell and draped over the cover.

She frowned. "What's wrong?"

He held the black disc in his hand, and after an awkward silence he said, "The Betrothal medallion… it's very important to you isn't it?"

10

Sam's sole aim now was to go to the site of the excavations and to the location where Emma and Paul had found the medallion. But she would take some persuading.

"Please Emm, I need you to do this one thing for me if I'm to lay this ghost to rest."

"But it's *my* medallion… mine and Paul's… it's all I have left of him," her pleas were almost childlike.

Something was telling him that he was already putting at risk this newfound trust she had given him. Maybe it was the tone of her voice, or the look in her eyes. He tried to reassure her.

"I just need it for a moment, just to talk with the spirit of the young soldier Arrian, and to find out what he wants, and to help him move on…to help *me* move on."

She gave in.

It was about twenty minutes drive north of Wraxbridge and on the edge of the open moor land. Just off the road, a loose-gravelled track way headed off towards the escarpment, on top of which could be seen the Great Wall. A steel gate with a sign in red letters saying 'Private: Site Closed. Keep Out' barred the way. As they pulled up, she stepped out, and opened the gate with a set of keys she produced from one of the deep pockets of her beloved overcoat.

She looked sad again, and spoke hesitantly.

"You go on alone," she said. "Follow your way along the track up the hill, and there you will find the excavations. You will see the parts of the wall we uncovered, which lead to the Mile castle. I'll wait here in the car."

Reluctantly, she handed him the medallion. She shivered, and once again huddled down into that huge, grey overcoat by burying her face into the lapels, and tucking her hair into the collar. Was it down to the brisk autumn breeze blowing over the moors, or was her grief was beginning to take hold again? She did manage a smile though.

"Take care up there," she said to him.

He nodded, and turned his attention to the climb.

When he arrived, nothing seemed out of the ordinary. It was as she had described; the remains of a segment of wall stood before him, about shoulder height, and about thirty to forty feet in length. The straight, rectangular arrangement of the stone brickwork, even after all these weather worn years, couldn't fail to impress. At the far end, the foundations of the Mile castle could be seen; a square building, perhaps ten feet in all directions, with an entire wall exposed. As he approached though, he could see that it was in a state of collapse. The police cordon tapes with the red and blue warning signs flickered in the breeze and betrayed the tragic accident that had befallen Paul Carter. What a waste.

But as he wandered from point to point with the medallion clasped firmly in his palm, he thought how peaceful it all seemed. He was looking for a sign… any sign. He gazed over the wall and ridge and to the bleak open valley to the north. It was devoid of trees and hedgerows and the only features that broke the ground were the Loughs – pools and lakes of water that reflected silver-grey against a heavily laden autumn sky. The season was definitely turning. A bracing cold breeze chilled him and made him shiver, and he wondered what it must have been like for a Roman sentry to look out from a turret such as this on a cold winter's day. The view, after all, had scarcely changed since those far off times.

It was at that very point – thinking of the Roman Sentry – when he sensed that he was no longer alone. At first he thought that Emma had had a change of heart, but he froze when he saw the figure, dressed in Roman armoury, looking at him from the far end of the segment of wall. For a moment he thought the figure was part of some historical re-enactment and he laughed to himself – trust him to pick such a day. He waved rather stupidly at the lonely figure, but it just stood and stared at him. But when he felt the black disc in his hand warm with a dull heat, it wasn't the cold that caused him to shiver. Until the incident at Edwulf's tower, he had never actually *seen* a spirit that had passed over before – he was simply able to sense their presence, or they had visited him in his dreams or visions. Now, it seemed to be happening often, and here, one stood before him – and in broad daylight too.

He had to see this through – to be afraid would be a mockery of his beliefs. With resolve, he walked towards the spectre. As he drew closer, the features on the figure became clearer; the shiny glint from the breastplate and rounded helmet, with its cheek guards, the grey-green tunic underneath, the bare legs, and laced footwear, and the sword in the sheath - all were as clear as day. And yet, when he tried to fix his stare on to the face, all he could see was a grey and translucent swirling mist.

The figure turned and started to walk away from him, heading down a slope towards lower ground. Sam quickened his pace but, by the time he reached the soldier's original position, he only had a moment to catch a fleeting glimpse of it as it disappeared into a hollow. Sam clambered down the slope with increased urgency but his clumsiness almost made him stumble. The ground was rain soaked and slippery underfoot, and cold water seeped into his shoes. Ahead, the sentry stopped in front of the ruined foundations of a tiny rectangular building, which was situated in a small depression of land. It appeared to hesitate before it crossed the threshold. Then it simply vanished.

Sam turned along a badly eroded footpath in the grass, and reached the hollow much quicker. A weather-worn tourist sign with the words 'Temple of Mithras, part of the fort of Proccolitia' lay broken on the ground.

The whole structure, he noticed, seemed to be sunken and below ground level.

The foundations of the building were only knee high, and the rectangular shape was no bigger than a bus. He stood by what he assumed to be the entrance – the point at which the soldier had disappeared. But the medallion remained warm and tingling in his hand, so he knew that his eerie companion remained with him – just the other side of the doorway he supposed. He sat down, took a deep breath and closed his eyes. All was silent, save for the numbing wind thudding in his ears.

Then, a voice called him and he opened his eyes. The building stood there in front of him - squat and low lying, but now it seemed new and complete, and capped with a neatly tiled roof.

"Thank the gods you have arrived Arrian. Don't just stand there, haul me out!"

He walked through the entrance and into an antechamber, which was only protected from the elements by a roof of wicker. Inside, a pit lay before him, where the voice had come from. A naked man held out his hand from the pit, which, it seemed, contained ice-cold water.

"Quickly man, help me; my time for the ordeal of penance is over."

It was obvious to Sam that he was inside the body and mind of Arrian again – the soldier who had led him there – he was seeing and experiencing things through his eyes and memory. He held out his hand and helped the man to his feet, and passed one of the rough towels hanging from the nearby rack to him. He recognised him as Pausanias. He was a small man but with a heavy squat figure and difficult to fell in combat he had no doubt. He was older, with a lined and sour face, but Arrian trusted him, as did all the cadets, because he looked after them, and introduced them to the cult of Mithras.

Pausanias dried himself with the towel, and talked while he did so. "Now listen to me Arrian my friend, before you enter the temple. The sullen look on your face tells me that you're worried about our actions on the night of the slaughter."

"Your actions, not mine."

"Listen I say. The enquiry as to what happened at the great stone circle is still going on; we all know the commanding officer's actions, though correct of course, haven't exactly made us popular with the locals. We killed many peasants that night thanks to your insight over that priest they call Cernunnos you befriended, but I think we'll be all right. As you can see, I've done my penance, and will now pray to Mithras for protection. The priests might even let me progress to the next grade – you know, the lion – for undergoing this ordeal by ice. You are still a raven... an initiate grade aren't you? Take another ordeal my friend, be part of the cult. Mithras will protect you on your travels, and in the next world as well!"

Then, in a more reflective tone, he continued, "Besides, I take comfort here in our small underground temple. We can pray for our fallen comrades for Mithras to protect them in the afterlife. What else have we got to look forward to, stuck out here for years on this miserable rain soaked land?"

"Hey, these are my people you know. I wanted no part in

that slaughter. It will haunt me for ever."

"Watch your tongue! They were your people Arrian, but no longer. It didn't stop you from enlisting did it? Like so many of your generation, lad, you've seen the benefits of joining the Roman army – but that means you are with us now. Anyway, it's not like in my day… I was drafted all the way from Dacia… but now that things have quietened down, they only want auxiliary troops like you, or a has been like me to patrol the frontier. Besides, they are simple peasants the lot of 'em, they'll mock you, rob you, and might even cut your throat if you're off guard. OK so we're at peace now, that's why there's only five hundred of us, just like any auxiliary unit, but it's our job to secure our part of the Wall, both as soldiers and law enforcers. That's all, that's our job. We collect the taxes, and in return they receive the benevolence and protection of our noble Emperor Marcus Aurelius."

After a momentary pause, he chuckled to himself. Arrian felt reassured by the wisdom of his older friend, but he didn't know whether he was being sincere or not. Pausanias continued to preach, "We respect the locals' ways but they pay homage to us, because they know that if they step out of line we can give 'em a bloody good hiding if need be! They won't argue – they know that while they're under our protection, they've got first pick of the trade over all other tribes around here."

They passed through a curtain, also made of wicker, and were plunged into darkness. This, they knew, represented the underworld – the cave of Mithras, who they believed, before life had begun, had slaughtered the bull, and released its life force for the benefits of humanity. From the bull's body grew plants and herbs, from its blood, came the vine, and from its semen, all useful animals.

Arrian knew all this, as he put on his headdress shaped like the raven, which was his grade, albeit a humble one. As his eyes adjusted to the gloom, he looked upon the mural painting on the far wall behind the altar – a painting of the god Mithras himself, slaughtering the bull. Beside the figure stood the sun god, who was his messenger, the moon goddess, and the raven – his raven. At his feet, a dog, a snake, and a scorpion assisted Mithras. Above were the words: 'Truth, Honour and Courage'. This whole mural, the Tauroctony as it was known, was encased in an egg-shaped frame, representing the womb from where Mithras was born, and was surrounded by twelve signs of the cosmos. All this was illuminated, and the colours brought to vibrant life by a beam of light emanating through a pinhole in a false wall, behind which shone several candles.

But, immediately in front of Arrian, stood the two main supporting pillars at the entrance. They were carved into the forms of Mithras' twin torchbearers, Cautes and Cautopates, representing the rising and setting of the sun, as well as hope and sorrow. They were also painted with vivid colours, and appeared alive and sentient by the illumination of the candlelight, which flickered in the darkness.

Yes, Arrian knew all this, but he also knew that he had to step forward and make an offering before he could take his place along side the others.

The room was dark and claustrophobic, and the sickly

smell of incense made him choke. It was difficult to see anything except for a row of seated figures – his fellow disciples, shrouded in robes and masks in the gloom. They seemed almost on top of him. Pausanias had left him, having joined the brethren where they sat.

Arrian knelt before the altar and plunged his hand into a deep, narrow wicker basket situated alongside. He groped around, until he had a firm grip on the warm struggling creature from within, and he winced at the pain caused by the sharp pecking on his hand. He hoisted the cockerel out, and with its throat firmly in his grip and its legs struggling feebly, he snapped its neck with a sharp twist of his wrist. He held the limp creature aloft, drew his dagger, and with a swift stroke, slit its throat and allowed the spurting blood to pour into a chalice upon the altar. After a few seconds, he tossed the lifeless form back into the basket, rose, and took his place among the benches.

But the gods were only to grant him a few moments of silence and contemplation. A disturbance of shouting, and what seemed like sticks clattering, and horses galloping sounded from somewhere outside. He sat there puzzled and frowned to himself as he waited for someone to take the initiative. Would no-one make a move? At last, the figure sitting near the entrance took off his headdress and disappeared through the wicker curtain.

"Gods, look at this!" the man yelled.

Pausanias was next through the curtain, with the three remaining men and Arrian following them; each threw their masks and headdresses aside.

For a moment the daylight blinded them, then Pausanias pointed to the sky and turned to Arrian with a broad, strangely euphoric grin appearing on his face, as if to say 'all is well'.

"Look Arrian, a raven, circling overhead – just like your – "

But he never finished his words.

The raven, like a heavy black sword, plunged from the sky and a muffled, then a winded sound came from the throat of Pausanias as he crumpled to the ground. A startled, wide-eyed stare had frozen on his face, and blood flowed profusely from his mouth. He was stone dead.

A woman stood over the body, with her foot grinding firmly into the dead man's chest, and with her blood-soaked sword still gripped in her hand. It was obvious to Arrian that she was one of the tribes' warrior queens from legend that he and his comrades had heard about, though they had never really believed in them. Morrigan, he thought they called her. Yes that was her name – Morrigan. He looked on in horror and for a second, just for a second, he recognised her as the naked female with the strange hair that escaped from the stones on the night of the sacrifice.

She had, Arrian thought, a figure a man would fight and die for, as was the fate of his friend Pausanius. Her face, partly hidden by the curled and spiky black hair blowing in the icy chill wind, turned to him, and for a moment her cruel and piercing eyes met his.

"You have killed our sister Brigit. I will have my revenge, and I will take her place and conceive your offspring, before I kill you."

He had no idea what she meant, but he had no time to mull over the words.

She drew her sword, and thrust it into the man standing alongside him, and withdrew it again in an instant. The man folded into a ball, clutching at his stomach and emitted a gurgling sound, before he collapsed to the ground in a lifeless heap. Arrian and the others stood transfixed in horror - startled and helpless. Then, another soldier swiftly turned and clambered up the steep bank behind the temple, but he didn't get far. He was cut down and engulfed by the hoard, which now surrounded them and their little den. With arms flaying, they chopped and hacked with their crude weapons at their victim, who, at least, was hidden from the soldiers' view.

A whole sea of painted war like faces stretched in all directions. They stared at them in a calm but eerie silence.

"Quick, inside, it's our only chance!" one of the remaining soldiers shouted, and all three survivors scrambled back into the dark bolthole.

Once inside, the same man spoke with authority. Arrian recognised him as Ando, a man from his own barracks.

"Help get these statues up against the entrance door," he ordered, and immediately he grabbed the stone figure of Cautes, and grunting and heaving, he dragged its bulk along the floor. "Rescuers must surely arrive soon."

Arrian and the other soldier assisted him. It was only after they had done this, and then dragged the other statue in order to complete the barricade, that it dawned on them that if the hostiles had wished to storm the temple, they would have done so by now. All three looked at each other distraught; fear filled their eyes and only their laboured breathing, broke the silence.

"Wait a minute!" Ando spoke. "What did she mean Arrian, when she said 'you have killed our sister Brigit'?"

Arrian shook his head, racking his brains. Then it dawned on him, and he gasped between breaths:

"Brigit... we were betrothed before I enlisted. She said something about wanting to die... surely she hasn't taken her own life like she said she would." Instinctively, he placed his hand inside his tunic pocket and onto the medallion – their medallion that sealed their betrothal to one another.

"Then it's you they're after," Ando retorted.

Panic began to well up in Arrian's stomach, "No, wait, they will kill us all..."

"Look!" the third man shouted, and put an end to the impending argument. He pointed to the ground. Smoke began to billow through the crevices of the entranceway. No barricade could prevent that. He sank to his knees, resigned and silent.

"Mithras will look after us in the afterlife. We've been good soldiers... it's been a good life, just so short, that's all..." he began to whimper.

"No way, no way, it's him they're after," growled Ando, and he leered at Arrian.

The smoke thickened and they started to choke, so Ando began to claw at the statues of Cautes and Cautopates, and then lunged at them frantically, as he shoved them with his shoulder. Eventually they toppled over with a resounding thud and clatter.

But he never got through the entrance. With the barricade made by the statues gone, a mass of burning bracken and wicker collapsed from outside and on to him. Quickly it took hold and smothered him with thick, black, belching smoke. His tunic caught fire, and as the smouldering red-hot mass began to cover and consume him, his blood curdling screams began to fade. But the others were too busy writhing around the floor to notice, as they coughed and choked and gasped for breath. Desperate to escape the smoke, they crawled passed the now silent smouldering mass of Ando's remains, to find air... cool, fresh air.

But their relief was momentary. The next thing he knew, Arrian felt what seemed like a dozen arms hoist him upwards and into the air. The light of day blinded him again. The barbarians were hauling him along at their shoulder height, and their triumphant yells and cries rang in his ears. Their hands clamped tightly around his arms, legs, and neck, and his chest was thrust out towards the sky. He was helpless as they carried him away from the temple, now rapidly disappearing into the small depression of land behind them. At least he was spared from witnessing his one remaining comrade's despatch into the afterlife – safely united once more amongst his fellows in the bosom of Mithras.

His mind was just able to register his betrothal medallion fall from his pocket and, as he was hauled into the air, the stream and grassy mound where he first made that betrothal to Brigit flashed momentarily before his eyes. But the noise of the mob closed around him as their grip around his body tightened. All he could see was the sky.

"Wake up... wake up... you must awaken Arrian... Arrian..."

His head ached so much and he felt sick. The room was going round and round, but just for a moment, he remembered who he really was – Sam Layton.

No harm would come to him, if only he could hang on to that very thought.

But there was no escaping the fact that his legs were pinned down, and when he struggled he could feel the bindings around his ankles and wrists tighten as they chaffed and cut against his flesh. But now the shouting in his ears had stopped and the sky had disappeared, and all he could see above was a roof of straw or thatch that enclosed him in darkness. He felt drugged. The crowds around his head remained, but they were out of his line of sight. Their chanting had replaced the shrieks, but it added to his sense of terror. Their strange words were not familiar to him, but as a drum began to beat, he remembered what happened at the stone circle. He felt his sweat trickle down his chest, and for the first time he realised that he was naked. Just then, something brushed by his feet, and he craned his neck towards them to see what it was. The female warrior, Morrigan, appeared once more, just as the fragrance of jasmine filled his head again; thick, heady and suffocating.

"Awaken Arrian. I wear her fragrance in memory of her." The chanting rose another pitch, "But you will not escape your bloodline, or your sacrificial destiny... I will take her place."

She loomed over him and straddled his waist and she lifted her tunic over her head to reveal her naked form. He knew what was going to happen, but despite the terror, he could not help himself. She leant forward, as her hair, and then her breasts brushed his chest. Her face filled his vision. Her fingers pressed on his lips and forced them open – he was too weak to resist. She forced something into his mouth, berries maybe, though he was unsure. Then she pressed hard on his jaw.

"Bite, bite on the elixir," she whispered.

A foul and bitter liquid hit the back of his throat causing him to convulse and cough, yet still she held him down with the grip of her flesh and thighs. The bitterness turned sweet and his head was swimming as he began to dream – to dream of Brigit and the night of his would-be betrothal. The drugs, the heat, and the stench of sweat, mingled with the heady jasmine, overwhelmed him. Her sighs and moans became more rapid, as she ground her hips into his.

"Your bloodline will stay with our people as you leave us."

The chanting became louder and more frantic. Her flesh was bathed in sweat, and her eyes were filled with blood lust as she bore down onto him, and at the same time a cold smile of contempt curled from her lips. The potion was wearing off as quickly as it had intoxicated him. He tried to hold back, but as his hands and feet were bound tight, he knew it was hopeless. There was no escape; he knew that – just as a drowning man, or a man dancing on the gibbet ceases his struggle, he then gave in too. When he felt the bittersweet surge welling up from within him, and into her, he knew it was over.

He was done with.

11

A voice was calling from somewhere distant. Sam was having difficulty recognising it, but as it drew nearer and became more urgent a face, blurred at first, began to form.

Emma's pale blue eyes studied him as she frowned. "Are you alright? Are you ill?"

Startled, he rose to his feet. Without a word he wiped the damp grass from his clothes. He still felt slightly disorientated, but she held out a hand to steady him.

"I saw you from the car. You appeared to be talking to someone in front of you, but there was no one there. Then you disappeared from view, so I thought I had better come looking for you... and here I found you, slumped by a mound on the grass. Are you sure you are alright?"

"I'm fine." He stood up straight, "But I am tired. How long have I been gone?"

"Just a short time, that's all."

"Time is relative," he muttered to himself.

"What?"

He shivered, but things were becoming more lucid again. He said, "Mind if we go back to your place for some hot soup or something?"

She grinned, now reassured, "Smooth talker!"

"I know."

His smile dropped as she turned her back and began the climb up the rise. Anxiously, he looked on the ground all around him, and then sighed with relief when he spotted the jet-black medallion lying on the grass.

***

Her apartment was actually situated on the third floor of a Victorian terraced villa, right at the top in fact. As they approached, something made them look skyward. They both caught sight of a huge dark bird, as it spread its wings, and launched itself from the rooftop. It soared into the air, silhouetted against the overcast sky.

"My God, a Raven," Sam pondered.

"Oh, is that what it is? I did wonder. It's been perched up there on and off for days now. It's odd because I thought I saw one at the village hall the other day."

They both stood in silence, and watched it fade into a dot as it flew into the distance.

She took out her key.

They sat at the kitchen table again, and he stirred the hot soup absent mindedly, whilst recounting the events that he had experienced. He concluded as he had begun, by shaking his head.

"Fascinating... I've been led by spirits before of course, but not to the extent of bonding with them, mind and body, and experiencing events from their life like that. It was so vivid."

"You should tell me about the dreams Sam, you hinted about them yesterday. You know, when you were small?"

He looked at her closely and sighed. He had been here before. He'd tell the people he grew close to all about them, but then they would leave him. Was this a scientist asking questions or, at last, someone he could put his complete trust in?

Her eyebrow was raised as though she were quietly expecting an answer. But there was tenderness in her voice. Now it was his turn to submit and to open up.

When he had finished recounting the terrifying visions his young mind had witnessed – the huge megaliths bearing down on him, the tower and the ticking of the clock, and the sickly smell of jasmine, along with the raven, it brought home to him just how all these elements had resurfaced in the last few months; ever since he had met Paul and Emma, and his recent associations with Forrester.

"You know," she replied, "through all the research I've done I can tell you that it's a pretty accurate description of what it must have been like back there, all that time ago."

"Go on." It seemed that his fear that she would look at him as one would look at a freak was unfounded.

"Well for a start, it sounds like the middle of the second century to me…you did mention the Emperor Marcus Aurelius… by that time the Wall was virtually complete and it was a relatively peaceful period of time.

The Wall was never meant to be patrolled regularly; it was, quite literally, a barrier to keep the barbarians out – besides, there was not enough manpower."

She smiled to herself, "The way you described the commanding officer – he sounds quite typical of the period – no military experience, and probably of minor royal lineage. It would be a quiet appointment, and he would be unlikely to receive another posting elsewhere... and the Wall was manned by Auxiliaries, in other words, second line troops of the Empire, just as your soldiers described."

She paused for a moment, lost in thought – her interest and imagination charged. She moved swiftly over to the bookcase and thumbed through the rows of books, picking through them and putting them back in place again as she continued:

"And each unit, in turn, was divided into Centurae, consisting of eighty men, not a hundred, and each was led by a Centurion...now they *were* fine officers who had risen through the ranks, and formed a professional core within the army. By that time most of the troops were locals – just like our friend Arrian, born in these lands, who saw the benefits of life in the army; you know, good pay and security, and, with luck, no major skirmishes!"

"But even so, why were there such a disparate group of men out there, away from the fort and open to attack, at that temple of Mithras or what ever it was called?"

"Oh, there's a whole host of reasons." Her confidence grew. "For a start, there's no evidence to suggest there were regular patrols in the first place. It could be that half, if not more of the unit were called away elsewhere – perhaps escorting and protecting supplies, both military and civil from the south. I would say that these men were policing the lands belonging to the Caledonians, making sure that their various tribal assemblies were benign."

"Well, the gathering at the stone circle wasn't exactly benign, nor what happened to me… that is I mean Arrian at the end."

"No, and that's where it gets really interesting," she enthused. "One of my books lists all the Celtic deities. It's in here."

She swiftly disappeared into the bedroom, and so he followed her. She sat on the bed and reached for a book by the table lamp.

"That name you mentioned, Morrigan, here she is, look!"

Sam had never seen her so fired up; all this was doing her good if nothing else – at last she had something to focus on other than grief.

She read out loud: "Celtic worship centred on the interplay of divine guardian spirits, often female, guarding the elements of nature in their lands – woodland, hills, streams and so forth, and their priestesses often came in groups of three. And they were not dissimilar to the Roman deities – Brigit – ah… that's interesting… was very like the Roman Goddess Minerva."

"But wouldn't the Romans have forbidden the worship of such cults?"

"No, not necessarily, they were tolerant of religious practices by and large. After all, it helped keep all the diverse peoples of the Empire acquiescent – let them worship their gods so long as Rome rules, that sort of thing. You could say it's how the British ran their own Empire eighteen hundred years hence. Besides, these Celtic Gods resembled their own gods and often became amalgamated; these lands became theirs, just as much as the indigenous population over time. By your soldier's time, that part of the Empire was administered and policed by the native peoples, so why shouldn't they turn to their own deities for divine guidance?"

He walked over and sat beside her on the edge of the bed.

"All this doesn't explain how I am to resolve my Roman infantryman's plight or, for that matter, his purpose for telling *me* his story."

"No... no indeed," she said, more quietly, and she closed the book and looked at him.

"Don't go chasing ghosts Sam, at least not at this moment. Stay… stay here with me."

She took the medallion still clasped in his hand away from him and placed it in the bedside drawer, but her hand remained closed around his. He just couldn't look away from her eyes; their gaze never left him – they took in a thousand messages and signs from his own heart and the sheer beauty of it touched him. She had complete trust in him, and he had never felt such a passionate longing for someone like this before.

Her face came closer, and without further reasoned thought he pulled her towards him and kissed her – lightly at first, but as she responded, her lips yielding, then her body, he wrapped his arms tightly around her. He wanted her. As his kiss became more intense, he caressed the small of her back, making it arch so that she was pressing herself against him. She gasped as she felt the passion well up inside him, warm against her stomach. His kiss moved from her open lips, to her cheek, to her ear, and a soft sigh rose from her bosom. She broke away, but left her hand in his, and drew back the bed cover.

***

When he awoke and opened his eyes, he noticed how the light coming through from the skylight above him was beginning to fade. It caused the shadows, as they flickered in the wind, to lengthen around the tiny bedroom.

"Late afternoon," he muttered. "It's getting dark already."

She stirred; her head was nestling against his shoulder, as she lay there all contented and sated with her eyes still closed.

"Mmm, it *is* autumn." Her lips formed a smile.

"Soon be November," he mused.

Her eyes opened, "Oh that's it!"

She pulled back the cover and reached over her side of the bed to retrieve the book that had been abandoned during their passion. He sighed with contentment as he took in her naked form. Her neck was so slender, her waist so narrow, and her skin so smooth and pale in the grey, fading light. All that feminine beauty had been hidden inside that thick, baggy overcoat.

She placed the book on her lap and brushed her soft hair from her face, as she began to read aloud again:

"The Celtic Goddess Morrigan – she represented a dark force of retribution that stood before the soldiers, and it describes her as a 'sultry, dangerous maiden', who, on the first of November, is said to have had intercourse with the War god Dragda, straddling a great river whilst she did so, and washing the blood from enemy soldiers' clothes yet to die in battle, combining it with the sperm of Dragda and giving birth to more warrior soldiers! Mm… gruesome! Maybe the date – the approaching anniversary – has something to do with the soldier's plight?"

"No, there's more to it than that… she was the form that Arrian witnessed flee from the carnage at the stone circle."

"Oh look, one more thing..." and her face dropped as her voice tapered off, as she continued to read:

"The Goddess often took the form of... a raven…."

Their eyes met. She shuddered, tossed the book aside, and nestled her warm body against his again. This was a kind of intimacy he had never known.

He looked around the room until his eyes rested on

a small and faded black and white photograph set in a thick wooden frame hung on the wall opposite them.

"What's that?"

"It's The Daughters of Carrawburgh stone circle," she said sleepily. "A very old picture taken in the nineteen twenties I think."

"Who's the woman in the picture?"

"Just one of the archaeologists; probably the same woman as you described from Edwulf's tower."

"No, I mean the other one in the background, in place of one of the megaliths."

She frowned. "But there's no one else. The circle in the photograph is complete, that's what makes it so unique. Now one stone is missing. Remember my diagram? I think you're seeing an optical illusion... the picture is old and faded after all." She sighed dreamily and closed her eyes again. "Just another mystery."

"But the figure... the long twisted ringlets of hair, just like Morrigan – it's blurred, and I'm sure she's looking at us." But his voice tailed off, for when he looked again, all he could see was the standing stones. Maybe it was the dim light playing tricks on him after all.

But he was uncertain. "Old photos like this fascinate me, especially when there's a face staring back at me... frozen in an instant of time from so long ago."

She chuckled and pressed her body against his. "You're funny... a dreamer, not like me. I'm a cold, matter of fact scientist, not taken to flights of fancy." She was teasing him.

Then they lay there in silence as exhaustion from the past few days overcame them, and they drifted off once more into a blessed sleep.

A glance at the bedside clock told him that he had been sitting beside her for an hour or more. Whilst she slept softly, he had remained restless and had propped himself up with a pillow against the headboard. And as his mind wandered, he stared at the shadows of a tree and its boughs and branches as they danced and swayed in the wind. Their silhouettes on the wall flickered and waved with each gust.

The soldier and the raven, and that awful sickly smell of jasmine, had haunted him since infancy, and it all centred around that medallion, treasured by the woman next to him – the woman who had put so much trust in him. He had worked out what he had to do before they had arrived back at the flat that afternoon. The spirit of the young soldier, Arrian, who had met such a violent death, would not rest until the medallion – the symbol of his betrothal – was returned to Brigit, his young lover. And she had been lying cold and dead somewhere under that grassy mound by the stream for nearly two millennia. Such manifestations, real or imaginary, would not go away. He *had* to chase these ghosts.

But for all of this, this cosy little room with its shifting shadows, and the gentle soft sighs coming from the sound asleep feminine form beside him, he would have been quite contented.

A clatter from the eaves broke his contemplation; the wind was picking up. The shadow of the tree became more animated, more frantic, as it danced in the gale. His eyes widened when he noticed the black outline of the bird again, this time perched at the end of the bough – he was certain that it was not there a moment ago. Of course, it was only a shadow, but it felt like it was staring at him – passing judgement.

The patter of the rain on the window made Emma stir; a momentary frown furrowed her brow as she turned over towards him, still fast asleep. Her naked shoulder was exposed, and it broke his thoughts as he stared at her pale soft skin again. The bough continued with the macabre dance, and the raven flew away, disappearing from the silent, luminous screen. Another clatter from the eaves made him look once more at the wall. There, the shadow of his soldier, the helmet, sword and sheath by his side, was clearly defined in the neon glow cast by the streetlight.

"Yes… yes..." he whispered to himself.

Finally he knew what he had to do. Quietly, he left Emma and the warmth of the bed and dressed, though all the while he could not take his eyes off her. She looked so contented and peaceful, and so loving. Taking the greatest of care, he opened the drawer by her side and retrieved the medallion. For a moment he held his breath as she stirred and the furrows on her brow returned, and a pang of despair shot through him over the act of betrayal he was about to commit.

He picked up her car keys and then crossed to the door. For a moment he hesitated, and turned towards her again. This was the one person who truly cared for him, and now he risked losing her. But, if he made this one sacrifice - the woman he loved - then these recurring hauntings should cease. It was a price he had to pay. He scribbled a note which simply said *'I'm so sorry. Please forgive me'* and left it on the kitchen table.

His plan was straightforward. He would drive back up to the site and await first light. Then, he would retrace his steps to the temple ruin, and with the help of his 'memory' of the young soldier's abduction, he would locate the stream and the mound where his young lover, Brigit, had lain for so long. When she had seen how much a part of the Roman army and its way of life Arrian had become, she had returned to their place of betrothal and taken her own life, and neither of their spirits had been able to rest ever since that time. It saddened him to think that they were so young and foolish, but he would give them back their betrothal medallion.

It would then only remain for him to return the car to the flat and quietly drop the keys through the letterbox. Then, he would collect his own vehicle, gather his belongings from his hotel, and head southwards and home.

And that is what he did.

The rain clouds and the gales had died and so, by the

time he reached the temple, the morning light diffused through the mist and blurred the landscape with colours of red and green, and it seemed so quiet and peaceful to him. Yet the noise of the mob that carried the soldier away screamed in his mind; two points of time set in the exact same location.

"Time is an illusion," he repeated to himself.

He thought about Arrian, and the path they took as they carried him along. He walked beyond the temple, and across the Vallum – once the huge ditch that led up to the Wall itself. Once he reached the Wall he could watch over the ridge to the north, where the ground sloped sharply away into the flat expanse of moorland below. On the other side of the Wall a rough footpath zigzagged its way to the bottom and towards a stream. A short distance away, a pool of crystal clear water glistened in the softness of the light. A large mound of grassed earth flanked its side. He knew that this was the path Arrian had taken almost two thousand years ago, as soldier and a captive when he was hauled away to his doom. He had recently trod the path through him. The terrain had not altered at all.

When he arrived at the pool, he paused and looked back at the ruins of the Wall on the ridge now above him. Except for the warmth of the summer sun, with its brightness in his eyes, the landscape had not changed since the day Brigit knelt at that spot, and playfully teased Arrian. Now, she lay buried and cold somewhere under that mound.

The pool of water appeared dark and deep, as the overhanging bank of earth cast a shadow. The medallion tingled in his hand. He took a last look at it and then tossed it into the dark pool. The 'plop' broke the stillness of the early morning air.

The spirits of the two young sweethearts could now rest but, as he slowly made his way back up the track way, all he could think about was Emma.

Winter

12

A cold blast of night air chilled the inn as the door swung open and the last of the guests arrived. With an awkward push and grinding noise the couple slammed the heavy oak door shut again, and silently mouthed an apology to the occupants of the room. It was already late, past 9pm and the crowd were anxious for proceedings to commence. As if treading on eggshells, the newcomers tiptoed their way to the last of the remaining unoccupied chairs at the back of the inn next to the bar.

This was the scene that Sam Layton looked on as he stood before the fire as it roared and glowed from the stone hearth. He looked over to the innkeeper, poised over the beer pumps, who wore a self-congratulatory smile as he worked. His idea about a spiritualist meeting drawing in the punters was certainly paying dividends; Wychwood inn had never been so busy. It was all in the tourist fly-leaflet, conveniently available at a dispenser near the bar:

'The perfect setting: a coaching inn dating to the seventeenth century, set on the edge of a sleepy town in the Cotswolds. Built of stone, and complete with oak beams and a thatched roof, a fine but nevertheless imposing Norman Church stands nearby. The church, set on a rise, dominates the medieval quarter of the town, and comes complete with a cemetery whose residents dated back as far as the War of the Roses.'

Such a setting was bound to conjure up its fair share of ghosts, of course, among which included the apparition of a white lady who frequented the churchyard on foggy nights, and the headless apparition of Anne Boleyn (who else) who drifted through the walls of the guest chambers on the first floor.

The bar was tightly packed with people as they squeezed and crouched onto the chairs next to the ancient, rough cut tables. Even the stools next to the bar spilled over with people. Sam was in no doubt as to how the innkeeper saw him: the star turn; the icing on the cake.

The room fell silent again and, with his customary broad smile, Sam glanced at the newcomers in his usual affable manner, and announced that they were welcome.

He paced a few steps from one side of the hearth to the other, occasionally facing his audience, and then he stopped and gazed at the centuries old portrait paintings on the walls. The red glow of the flickering firelight caused the faces to move and come to life, or at least that's how it seemed.

He waited for the spirits to touch him just as they always did, but his momentary pause grew longer; this time nothing filled his mind, save for an empty silence – nothing was coming through from the other side. He was tired, that much was true, and he could not stop thinking about Emma – these things were clouding his mind for sure. He had not appreciated how his love for her had grown until now. After his act of betrayal over the medallion, he had just run away. It was the easy thing to do. "Out of sight, out of mind," he told himself over and over.

Then the note came – delivered to him via his agent's address and sent on to him, almost as an afterthought. "Just another hanger on," the agent had said as she handed him the sealed envelope. "You shouldn't become so personally involved Sam, you know that."

How could he not be personally involved?

Without even being conscious of the act, he nervously fingered the now crumpled note that he had carried in his inside pocket all through the long cold winter months. He knew the words by heart:

'Dearest Sam,

Your note was an awful way to say goodbye.

You should know how hurt and betrayed I feel at your stealing my betrothal medallion, which was so precious to me, especially as I put so much trust and faith in you, as well as allowing you into my bed. For what it's worth though, I do forgive you because I understand your motives.

I think we both need to move on. For my part, now that I

am over the grieving, I have decided to continue with the excavations that Paul and I were involved with, provided that I can get some of the old team back together. I owe it to him. Mr Forrester continues to call me. He wants me on board and says I've a vital role in his research. Flattery I expect, but for what purpose? Anyway, I need the money.

I wonder if we shall meet again.

Take care,

Love Emma.'

He thought back and smiled to himself as he recalled with affection the small figure hidden in the grey overcoat, and the straight fair hair as it cascaded over the lapels - and those pale blue sorrowful eyes. He remembered how they met and that golden day they spent together in Wraxbridge. Where was she now?

A shuffling of feet and a cough from the audience broke his reverie. A moment of alarm replaced his thoughts – where were the spirits? Why were they not travelling over from the astral plane?

For the very first time, the notion of bluffing his way through occurred to him.

"Er, does the letter 'L' mean anything to anyone?" This was the way of the charlatan. His hesitancy would betray him.

His gaze wandered among the sea of expectant faces in desperation, that is until it fixed on a figure that sat by the wall, just in shadow behind an oak beam post. He thought how odd it was that he had not noticed it before, and curious that it seemed detached from the rest of the crowd – as if it did not belong there.

Then it dawned on him, and the alarm bells sounded. Forrester!

He had dreaded this moment. Forrester was the scourge of all spiritual mediums. He had no empathy, spiritual or otherwise with Sam's fraternity, and turned up at gatherings such as these purely to cause trouble, or as Forrester would put it, 'To expose the fraudsters for what they are – fakes, and charlatans!' And furthermore, he had never bothered so much as to contact him since that night at Edwulf's tower, and he'd therefore cause to look over his shoulder ever since.

So now it was the time of reckoning. He sat there, straight-backed and imposing, and resting both gloved hands on a silver tipped cane. His black trench coat was unbuttoned, revealing a suit and tie, and his eyes, dark and accusing, stared back at Sam. His short dark wavy hair, greying at the temples, and his aquiline nose added to his aristocratic air. None of Sam's friends knew anything about him, but his very presence at gatherings such as these always put paid to any communion with the spirit world.

Sam had scarcely a moment to contemplate this awful turn of events before his attention turned towards the heavy oak door as it screeched open once again. Everyone turned and gasped in unison. This time the door seemed to have opened by its own accord, for no one could be seen to enter. An icy, echoic blast of wind whistled through the inn, and caused further simultaneous gasps of shock amongst the crowd. Quickly, the innkeeper moved from behind the bar and slammed the door shut once more.

"Er... now, again, I'd like everyone to... er, clear their mind... if you please."

Sam was struggling to regain control of the situation, but what he then saw at the back of the audience effectively ended any chance of salvaging the situation.

A figure stood in the shadows of the dim flickering light, far away by the troublesome door. It stood in a huge grey overcoat, and the small face, strangely pale and glowing by the light of the bar, appeared to be staring impassively back at him, even though he could not make out the features.

"Emma!" He spoke the name out loud as his hand clasped the crumpled note now back in his pocket.

The murmurings among the restless crowd began again.

A splinter of wood crackled in the hearth and made him look away, but when he turned back again the image had vanished. His heart pounded as his troubled mind tried to make sense of the situation. He hurried towards the door, pushing into the crowd, and as they rose to give him room, he knocked into the chairs making them crash onto the hard stone floor. He scarcely acknowledged their indignant cries as he made his way to the exit.

Once outside, he strained his eyes as they tried to adjust to the darkness. A bright moon cast deep shadows all around, making it even harder for him to see.

"Emma...Emma!" he called out as the pale vapour of his breath dissolved into a silent, cold night air.

His searching came to a halt in the direction of the churchyard; just for a moment, a slight movement from the corner of his eye held his attention – a wisp of something gliding along the pathway amidst the gravestones – some shape, pale white and luminescent and shrouded in an outer garment – a cloak, or gown perhaps. It appeared to be moving away from him. Instinctively, he sprinted into the churchyard. His footsteps seemed to echo around the gravestones and walls of the church in the still night, and it caused the apparition to stop and turn. All of a sudden, it dissolved behind a low wall, blackened by shadows caused by the moon. A trick of the light? He wasn't sure. When he hurried towards it, he discovered that he was looking upon a gravestone hidden behind the wall – the shape must have vanished behind it, but it was too weather worn and covered in lichen for him to decipher, especially in the poor light.

Just then, the ornamental lights that illuminated the imposing walls and tower of the church were extinguished, and he was plunged into blackness. Temporarily disorientated, once more he had to wait for his eyes to grow accustomed. The only light he had to guide him now was that of the moon as it cast its deep shadows onto the yew trees and gravestones. Luckily, the moonlight reflected on icy particles formed by the frost on the ground and so acted as a guide along the narrow, winding path. What was he doing, thinking about such things? Surely Emma – the figure in the overcoat – was not the same as this ghostly shape that had led him to this gravestone.

He laughed to himself cynically. So, the ghostly apparition said to walk among the churchyard near Wychwood Inn really did exist. So what, it meant nothing to him – in fact he considered it to be quite ordinary.

The fact was, Emma was lost to him; he cursed at his stupidity.

He called out her name once more, but more to himself really. Realising the situation was hopeless he walked aimlessly around the pathways of the churchyard, before finally coming to a halt in front of the huge arch of the north door. The church clock struck eleven and he shivered. It was bitterly cold and his eyes and ears stung. He realised that he hadn't even got his coat. Soon the revellers would be pouring out of the hostelries from the nearby market square, and the stillness of the night would be shattered.

Slowly, and with a heavy heart, he began to retrace his steps back to the inn. Hopefully the audience that he had failed would be making their way home by now, and with any luck, he would not have to cross the path of the Innkeeper, at least not until the morning. He would sneak up to his room, and retire for the night.

That was the only thing that went according to plan all evening.

***

As he tossed and turned in the uneasy realm that existed between his waking and sleeping mind, a strange light began to diffuse through his eyelids. A curious thought began to form in his semi conscious mind that this was not how it should be; he knew that he had turned out the bedside light before going to sleep.

So he opened his eyes. All around him, the whole bed was bathed in a pale and diffused white light. Something soft and feminine stirred beside him. He frowned. It didn't make sense, but Emma was with him; they were together once more. Her back was towards him, but he placed his hand on her shoulder, and brushed his face against her delicate, soft hair, and breathed in her fragrance. The sensual and intimate sensation from the warmth of her nakedness filled his senses, and overcame him as he sank further into the bedclothes.

This wasn't real. How could it be?

She stirred, then turned and pressed her face close to his so that he could feel her breath. She mounted him and then he wrapped his arm around her shoulders and into the small of her back, as he pulled her tightly into him. Her body yielded to his strength, and she sighed with contentment as she softly kissed his ear. Their bodies locked together as they embraced ever more tightly as their lips met. He gently held her head, kissed her on the lips, and then her forehead, and gazed into the bright vividness of her eyes – so close he could see into her soul. She sighed again as she smiled, and nestled her head on his shoulder. He kissed and stroked her. The warmth of her breast pressed against him, and he felt her heart beating through his own – and he could hear it too, pounding and beating on his chest.

At that very moment, she suddenly raised her head, looked into his eyes, and cupped the palm of her hand on his cheek.

"This is not a dream," she whispered softly.

A sudden feeling of terror, like a shockwave, seared through him as the light blotted out; all was dark, and all he could see was her face – startled, and with a twisted look of pain. She lurched back, and appeared to fall away and towards the ground – except there was no ground to fall into. The blood rushed to his head as he felt himself tumble after her, down, down, into a dark chasm where no light shone. There was nothing but inky blackness all around, until suddenly they came to a halt with a sickening thud, and the sound of bones cracking and snapping. A muffled cry of pain gurgled from her throat as he looked on in horror at her broken body, then he too crashed to a halt on top of her. All he could see was her face close to his. Blood trickled from her mouth. She seemed pinned down, but he staggered to his feet. As his head swam, a mist enveloped him, but he could still make out the damp, dew-soaked grass that he stood on, and the weathered standing stone that towered overhead where her broken body lay. In a great effort, she managed to open her mouth and raise an outstretched arm, though she was too winded and broken to cry out.

A knocking sound resonated from the stone, and as it grew louder, a figure – its face masked and cloaked in a shroud – appeared beside it at the same time. It held a cane, or rather a bone from a leg or limb, and it was tapping it rapidly against the megalith.

Then a thudding sensation shook through his body, and Emma let out another winded cry. The ground had opened up, and she began to sink into the clammy, wet grass. Then came more of the tapping, followed by another body-shaking thud, and a further cry, though this time more feeble. As she sank into the earth, and the grassy turf and clay enveloped her still further, all he could see was her head and one remaining arm outstretched – and her mouth open in a look of silent despair – all that was left of his beloved Emma. She sank beneath the standing stone as it consumed her.

Tap...tap...tap....

The tapping became louder and incessant until it filled his brain and that was all he could hear. He could no longer see anything except for mist – that is, until conscious reasoned thought began to return to him.

Tap...tap...tap....

Still it continued, but now he realised. He reached out, and fumbled for the light switch. The darkness was over. His body was drenched in sweat, and his breathing heavy.

"Emma!"

He reached over to the other side of the bed. She wasn't there, of course not, it had just been a god-awful dream. Then the terrible thought occurred to him; that was how many of the spirits called to him – through his dreams, right back from when he was a child lying ill on the settee. He thought of the young Roman soldier again and how he first came to him through dreams. He groaned in despair.

Emma's dead. He knew it.

Still the incessant tapping continued. He strained his ears as he tried to locate the source, until he realised that it was coming from the door. He turned over to face the alarm clock. It was 2a.m.What the hell was going on?

He groaned again and rubbed his eyes as he stepped out of bed, put on his dressing gown and slippers, and walked over to the door.

"Who's there?" he croaked.

"Forrester. Do hurry up and let me in old chap, I'm not going away and that's that!"

Filled with apprehension, he opened the door. Sure enough, the towering figure of Forrester stood before him.

"What do you want?" Sam stammered. "And how on earth did you get through the main door and up the stairs without being noticed? The landlord... the staff...."

He peered beyond the giant, out into the dimly lit landing and corridor. All remained still and quiet; not another soul had been disturbed. Maybe the light was playing tricks and he was still half asleep, but it was as if Forrester did not really exist there – no-one else would register his presence.

"How on earth indeed!" the man scorned. "The landlord's just another imbecile in my employ. I arranged the whole charade this evening. Easy peasy, you might say, that is until for some mysterious reason you ran away."

His grin was menacing and humourless.

"But, look, that's not important. Mind if I come in? 'Course you don't!" He gave Sam no time to reply.

He gestured with the silver-tipped cane, the obvious source of the tapping noise, for Sam to stand aside, and pushed him back across the threshold. From the inside pocket of his trench coat he pulled out a bottle of malt whisky.

"Time for a philosophical discussion I think. Believe me, we have plenty to talk about. Er, glasses old chap?"

Forrester looked around him, and noticed a small dining table with two chairs beside the curtained window.

"We'll sit over there I think, well it will have to do won't it?" he sniffed. "I must say you do look ridiculous standing there, mouth agog, clad in jim-jams, so be a good fellow and fetch the glasses."

Sam could do nothing but acquiesce. Forrester's well-spoken and faintly arrogant manner mirrored his appearance – well-dressed, elegant, almost aristocratic, self-assured, and therefore highly assertive. Even when he sat down he remained an imposing figure.

Sam fumbled for a couple of glasses from the nearby sideboard and handed them to Forrester, who proceeded to pour. He could not help but notice how he deftly undid the buttons on his driving gloves to reveal the rich dark, jewel-encrusted rings that he wore on his long, neat fingers.

"What do you want Forrester?" Sam steeled himself. "You managed to kill off the proceedings well enough this evening, so what more do you want? Come to gloat?"

The slight snide and self-assured smirk never left Forrester's face.

"Not at all old boy. Yes it's true, I despise all of you so called spiritualists, and I won't hesitate to expose the cowboys and the fraudsters among you, but that's not the reason for my being here. I have every faith in *you* old chap, but like so many of your peers, you waste your powers; you fritter away your time contacting the recent dead, passing on personal messages back and forth from this spiritual plane to the next – all sentimental claptrap, and it never occurs to you about the potential that you *could* tap into."

Sam realised now that there was a great deal more to this man than a mere sceptic, and the look on his face must have urged Forrester on.

"Oh, I know all about you and your ghostly goings on with the sweet little Celtic girl and her lost love for The Roman soldier boy... all very touching, I'm sure."

"How can you possibly know that?"

"It doesn't matter. And I'll forgive you for that... shall we say... indiscretion at Edwulf's tower with Carter." Then his face suddenly darkened and his smile, albeit a false one, dropped. And it chilled Sam as his eyes flashed jet-black: "And for your failure and subsequent deception over your psychic findings at the stone circle."

But then his expression lightened again, and he began to study his wrists and manicured fingers in a way Sam had noticed before.

"Look, just imagine if you could tap into the collective minds of many generations of the dead going back not just a generation or two, but over millennia, and all at the same time too. Think of the concentrated psychic energy that would exist within such a pool... think of the knowledge, the wisdom and the *power* that you would hold."

"That's got nothing to do with me."

"Oh but it has my dear Layton, it has. Your... associate, if that is the appropriate term, Emma Carter?"

"What's that got to do with you? What's become of her?" He was becoming more agitated.

"Well that's just it old chap, I don't know, so you see that's what we have in common. We are both anxious to trace her whereabouts."

"I don't understand."

"She's vital to my work at the stone circle. I need her for one more thing, and now she has disappeared. To put it bluntly, I believe she's dead, and so do you, don't you?"

"You're not known for your subtlety are you?"

"I need to know for sure Layton, and soon, but for reasons that don't concern you; and that's why I need you to contact her, either in this world or the next."

Sam gulped down his whisky at the thought of the dreadful finality of it all.

"Then I need to know more about this stone circle she was working on," and he thrust out his glass for another helping. Forrester obliged.

"Very well." Forrester became more contemplative, his voice more slow and cautious. "A little history lesson won't do any harm I suppose. Are you sitting comfortably? Then, I will begin."

Forrester's self-assured smirk returned and he sat back, whisky in hand, and looked towards the ceiling and walls as he spoke:

"The Daughters of Carrawburgh stone circle, as we like to call it, lies on the Cumbria-Northumberland border, about two miles to the west of Hadrian's Wall. The Irish Sea can be reached a further five miles beyond. All of the surrounding land has been owned by me for millennia – "

"You mean by your ancestors," Sam corrected.

"Not exactly." Forrester's eyes narrowed and his voice slowed. Sam wasn't sure whether it was through indignation at the interruption, or for another reason hidden to him, but Forrester returned to form and continued with his lecture:

"The circle is one of the largest henges that we know

of, and dates from the late Neolithic period, and it is reckoned that the megaliths were brought there from around four thousand years ago. The henge, or the ring and ditch, as you would call it, are probably a thousand years older.

"The megaliths themselves, which consist of a kind of roughly hewn sandstone, were almost certainly brought from the three foothills that lie to the east. Interestingly, during the darker winter months, one cannot help but notice how, when the constellation of Orion the hunter rises in the east, the three bright stars in a row that form his belt align themselves with those hills – as well as the three massive portal stones that form the eastern entrance. This was the time of year when they believed that the dead travelled to the underworld, the afterlife – "

Sam had held out the palm of his hand, making a clear sign for Forrester to stop.

"Yes, yes alright, but this isn't helping me to find Emma is it?"

"Oh come now, a chap like you, in touch with the spirit world, not interested? 'Course you are! Ever wondered how the circle acquired its rather quaint name?"

Sam emitted a sigh of resignation, and without waiting for a reply, Forrester continued:

"Take the 'Merry Maidens' of Cornwall, or the 'Nine Ladies' of Derbyshire for instance; girls, virgins and so on, who have supposedly been turned to stone for dancing on the Sabbath. We assume these folk stories are no more than fairy tales, and are merely obstructions in our quest for the truth. After all, our medieval friends – the monks, scholars and so on – were our earliest historians, but in all their ignorance they would not have a clue where these fanciful names originated… except from folklore."

Sam thought back to Emma's description about the origins of the name 'Daughters of Carrawburgh' and it's dark connotations. It seemed to tie in. He shuddered at the thought, but Forrester seemed oblivious as he continued:

"This notion of maidens rhythmic dancing to music, and the resultant sexually charged energy, is widespread throughout our island. Since we know that rings of standing stones were used in ritual dancing in other parts of the world – Africa, the far-east, as well as Europe – then surely these mystical names provide a clue to the activities that took place here in antiquity. No doubt our distant ancestors saw these rituals as an offering to ensure fertility... the fruitfulness of the land, and of their offspring – acts which the early Christians saw as obscene and blasphemous."

The expression on his face darkened once more, but the humourless smile remained.

"Yes, it's incredible that these folk-tales lasted for so many generations by word of mouth, especially when you consider how the Christians would have attempted to expunge it from the people's consciousness. Just imagine what the megaliths could tell you if they were alive, if their thoughts could be transmitted..."

This last point was lost on Sam; this was not getting him anywhere. Weariness was beginning to overwhelm him – that and the heady effects of the booze. All he could think about was beautiful Emma.

"I thought I saw her tonight, back there..."

Forrester's lecturing ceased, and for the first time, his self-assuredness dropped. His eyes widened, and the ever-menacing air lurking behind the false veil of charm, surfaced.

"You saw Emma Carter tonight? So she's not dead…"

"No, that's not what I mean. I saw an image... she's trying to communicate, so maybe she *is* dead, I don't know."

Forrester rose suddenly, and slammed the half empty bottle of whisky onto the table in front of Sam. He reached for his cane, and placed it on Sam's shoulder. Instinctively, Sam turned to the malignant stare of the suave man, and was transfixed like a startled rabbit.

"Sleep now," Forrester commanded. "But I require you to find her; dead or alive. I *must* find the whereabouts of that woman."

His cool self-assuredness returned. He buttoned his coat, and without another word, he walked to the door and made his exit.

Puzzled, agitated and confused, Sam stumbled from his chair and followed. The corridor and landing remained silent and undisturbed in the dim, shadowy light. There was no sign of Forrester – as though he had never been there.

"Sleep now" Forrester had said but how could he?

A visit by that man at the dead of night would put paid to that even under normal circumstances, but Forrester's cold and unfeeling bluntness over Emma's demise on the very night he saw her, or an image of her, whatever it was, just made him curse at his dithering.

He thought back to his childhood, and to the visions and phantoms that frightened him as he lay on the settee, as his mother sang her lullaby from so far away in the kitchen.

13

It was late afternoon and so already dark by the time Sam had arrived in Wraxbridge. He had plenty of time to think during the long drive north. He had stopped off at a couple of service stations for rest and refreshment, but was no nearer in forming a plan of action, other than to return to Emma's apartment and look for clues – any clues.

A heavy mist had descended and the still air was so cold that it chilled him to the bone. How different it had all seemed here just a few months ago when the autumn gales stirred everything to life around him. But all of that might as well have been a hundred years ago.

When he climbed the steps to the third floor of the Victorian terraced building, the absurd thought occurred to him that it was all some sort of elaborate joke designed to punish him for his actions, but the hollow echo of his footsteps against the concrete stairs brought it home to him; there was no life here. He was alone.

It was time to put on his trademark smile and knock on a couple of doors to the apartments below, he told himself. But then he thought better of it.

Assuming that she had disappeared, he would have to gain entry to her flat by stealth, in which case the neighbours would probably hear his movements from the floor above. No, it was best not to advertise his presence within the building.

Still, it hadn't occurred to him as to how he would actually gain entry to her apartment, but then the problem never arose; to his surprise, he found the door unlocked. Feeling alarmed, for a moment he hesitated; perhaps she had left in a hurry, or someone had been here before him. If so, were they still here? Judging from the silence and darkness from within, he decided he was quite alone and so, with an involuntary glance over his shoulder to reassure him that he wasn't being watched, he stepped over the threshold.

He stood immediately on the other side of the door and listened intensely for any sound – anything at all that would betray any other presence, but the stillness held. The misty orange glow from the streetlights filtered through the tiny windows of the kitchen and sitting room area, and although he could barely make out any of the room's features, he felt safe. He could relax a little.

He walked over to the windows, drew the curtains and then switched on as many lights as he could. He clicked the door shut so as to lock himself in and lit the fire. Soon the air began to warm him through. Now the room, the armchairs, the bookcase and the rest of the furniture seemed welcoming, and he thought back to his cosy tryst with Emma and their intimacy with longing. She belonged here; *they* belonged here. Where was she?

He shivered and he wrapped his arms around his shoulders. It was still cold in here; she had not occupied the flat for some time. The pile of unopened mail by the letterbox confirmed his thoughts.

He was tired too. He would make himself a meal from whatever he could find in the cupboards and then sleep. He would dream about the past, and then in the morning, when he was refreshed, he would look for clues. Just for a moment he kidded himself – perhaps she would walk through the door at any moment.

After he had finished his meal, he picked up the unopened mail and, without much purpose, he sifted through the bills and junk mail until one item – a large manila envelope with a hand written address – caught his attention. He tore it open. It contained a few loose and crumpled pages that appeared to be extracts from a diary. He only had to read the first few lines to realise that it was *her* diary. No time to question why it had arrived there. At last, there was something to go on, and perfect bedtime reading! He switched off the lights and retreated to the bedroom. As he rested against the headboard of the bed he turned to the crumpled but precious pages written by Emma:

'These notes made for my personal diary, I will use when I go home to Wraxbridge at the end of the week. They will help me to put a more three dimensional slant on my archaeological journal, which I shall of course keep separate. I am pleased to say that I have managed to assemble some people from Paul's old team, so we should be able to adopt a reasoned, scientific approach to the dig, along with any finds and discoveries we may make. There is another individual with us by the name of Hobson who I recognise as the proprietor of the inn where I am staying. He's a dour man with little charm, and everything

seems too much trouble for him. I don't really know what his role is, but he tells me that Mr Forrester employs him. I suggested to him that we enlist the help of some students who are working on a project just north of here, as any increase in manpower would be helpful given Forrester's demanding time scales, and I'm sure they would welcome the experience of a dig, but Hobson stated that Forrester was keen to employ as few people as possible. He did mention that a colleague of his would be joining us though, to help 'oversee matters'. Funny, I thought that was my job.

SUNDAY

On the first day, Hobson and this other guy escorted me from the inn and drove me to the site, and announced that they were to be my chaperones for the duration. I suppose it makes sense. My car's hardly designed to negotiate the rough terrain that leads to the stone circle. Gone are the days when Paul and I could come and go as we please.

There was no sign of my team but I was assured they would be joining us the following day, and that they were busy collating the geophysical and landscape data already held at the university. There was no chance of contacting them since there was no signal to be had on my mobile – not in this remote spot.

The other man's name was Gunter, a surly looking individual I must say.

Anyway Paul and I had already recorded the basic layout and constituents of the site and its position in situ to the land. The circle of stones consists of thirty-two megaliths varying in shape and size, the details of which I recorded, but they followed the usual sequence of tall 'masculine' shapes to that of the more rounded 'female' variety. It's still astonishing to think that only one of the latter forms are missing, yet, when I remember back to the old photograph on the wall, it shows the circle as complete. I remember Sam pointed that out to me…

Involuntarily, Sam looked up at the wall and to the hanging picture frame hidden in the lamplight.

Basically I think it's an illusion, and the stone has been lost in antiquity. It has become known locally as the Alnilam stone, for reasons I cannot fathom – though I remember Sam mentioning that name when telling me of his psychic experiences on the night of the sacrifices and of the Romans. Other than that, the circle does appear to be complete. Quite a find!

Mr Forrester insists that the circle dates from the late Neolithic, and judging by the size and circumference of the near perfect circle, he's probably right. It lies on a gently sloping plateau with mountains on the far horizon in all directions. Nearby, there are foothills and fells with the distant hills to the east forming a row. There are entrances to the circle at all four compass points, but the east entrance is particularly striking as there are three huge monoliths forming a portal. This was probably used for rituals and ceremonies. The land I suppose would have been cleared of forest around the time the henge was constructed – a far earlier time than the stones, so the terrain that I am looking on now is relatively unchanged. The soil is soft and damp, yet firm, just as you would expect at this time of year, and so in spite of the shorte,ss of daylight and the cold, I am not expecting any difficulties when I start excavating tomorrow, though quite what I'm looking for, I do not know.

Still, it makes sense to reappraise the whole site, what with the grisly murder last summer, we never really had the chance to develop our work here.

MONDAY

Today I encountered my first problems, though not so with the weather! It remains bright and sunny though bitterly cold, but the bright winter sunlight allows me to enjoy the views of the surrounding fells.

No, it's the personnel that are proving to be a problem. Hobson remains as dour and unhelpful as ever; anything I ask him to do is either too much trouble as 'he has his hotel to run', or is 'not within his remit' as he puts it. Gunter is a rough individual who I don't much care for – he is just a big, thuggish oaf and he hovers over me as if he has instructions not to let me out of his sight. Neither man shows much interest in archaeology, or possess any of the basic skills, and I wonder for what purpose Forrester employs them. I was disappointed not to hear from the team back at the university. That is something I will have to address tomorrow.

TUESDAY

Things looked up today, or at least it started out that way! Megan, who's now working at the reception desk of the hotel, handed me a note. It was from Paul's former colleagues at the university. They shall return tomorrow. That's good! Also, my two minders took me to the circle, and then drove off and left me there. Even better!

From my research, I knew that the oak tree that grows at the centre of the circle stands on the site of a barrow, which is said to pre-date the circle by some degree, but the mound has long since disappeared. However, amidst the trunk and protruding roots, I could determine the remains of a cove of stone forming three sides of an open square. This, I am sure, belongs to the entrance of the lost barrow.

As luck would have it, the students descended on me at that very moment. There were about six guys and lasses and, although they were a bit boisterous, I was glad of their company and it reminded me of my carefree university days when I met Paul. A few of them I remember from the dig at the Roman bridge on the river. It turns out that they are on a field trip or gap and are helping out at an iron age re-enactment camp over on the nearest of the foothills – experimenting with the construction of iron age farming, pottery and weaving, that sort of thing. They told me a bit about the local history, especially how the Romans put the tribes people to the sword with such savagery, but for reasons unknown. They had also read somewhere that this was about the time that the so called Alnilam stone went missing, well that ties in with Sam's experiences.

Sam looked up from the notepaper and as he stared into the dim light of the bedroom, he thought back to the visions he saw through Arrian on the night of the sacrifice. Then, he continued to read:

Anyway, to my delight, the students were keen to lend me

a hand with the excavating. I showed them how to dig beneath the megaliths in order to look for the remains of burnt offerings and fragments of bone and so forth, whilst I and a couple of the others could concentrate on the area around the oak and the cove.

We did this for a few hours until Hobson and Gunter returned, but what they did quite upset me. They told the students in no uncertain terms to leave, and stated that it was private land and that they would be 'sorted out' if they returned. I can well remember Gunter grinding his fist in his palm with his top lip curled. His eyes were filled with thuggish hate as he issued his threat. As they left, some of them ventured a wry smile in my direction, as well as a few rude gestures towards Gunter when the oaf's back was turned. They wished me luck as they departed.

I was alone again and, ridiculous as it may sound, I felt like a prisoner. By now the light was beginning to fade and I was faced with a choice: a lift back with these two, or a long cold walk to the inn. I chose the former option but I didn't like their company; not one bit.

I do feel alone. I ate little this evening and just sat in silence in the bar playing with my food. Save for a few locals who keep themselves to themselves, no one seems to visit the bar. I know it's only a small hotel, but still! I was half hoping that the students would pay a visit as their bonhomie would have cheered me up, but it never happened.

WEDNESDAY

On cue, my minders escorted me back to the dig this

morning. It was awful because now they seemed more determined than ever not to let me out of their sight. All they seemed interested in was for me to confirm the existence of burnt offerings of human bone under each and every one of the megaliths. I told them we'd been through all this last summer. 'Mr Forrester's instructions' they insisted. When I happened to remark that one was missing anyway, Gunter just smirked and said the vacancy was for me, but then Hobson nudged him in the ribs for him to stop. I think he got a kick out of trying to frighten me.

It was exhausting and very cold, and following another crude remark from Gunter saying that the fires would warm me up or something, I insisted that unless they mucked in, I would never finish the job given Forrester's urgency over it all.

That said I tried to remain objective and scientific. I traced fragments of human bones amidst petrified ash under each and every one of the stones. I worked like a slave, taking few breaks for sustenance, and only at my further insistence due to the fading light did we call it a day. I just wanted a meal and a long hot soak.

Tonight as I write this in my room, I have had time to think and I'll admit that I am frightened.

Someone has been in here. For one thing my mobile phone is missing. At first I thought that I must have left it at the dig, but when I returned from the bathroom along the hallway, my door was ajar, and I know *I locked it. My laptop is also missing, which contained my journal and all my hard work, and I left it right here on the bed. Who can I complain to since it's obvious that one of the staff must have had a passkey? I can hardly go to Hobson. And worse is that the wardrobe has been cleared out so that I have no clothes save for the bathrobe that I am wearing. In short, I have no means in contacting the outside world. I should have sensed the danger following the disappearance of the team. Why have they not been in touch? I could kick myself for being so naÏve.*

Yes, this is turning into a nightmare, and I'm frightened. So much for fat pay cheques and easy money. I have resolved, therefore, that at first light I will find Megan, for she's the only one who I can call a friend. She can lend me some clothes, and I will drive away, just disappear. If I go now, Hobson is bound to notice, but if I leave at first light, he might not miss me.

As I write, I can hear raised voices from the stairs. I'm sure it's Gunter and Hobson, so I'll retire now – shut myself away. I do feel rather afraid and lonely. If I can only get through the night.

And that was it. No more.

"Just a few fragments of scribble, nothing else!" He cursed to himself involuntarily as he frantically re-read the lines in a useless attempt to find something that he may have missed. There was mention of a Megan. He remembered that name from the note Emma had passed to him when he first met her – so it was obviously someone she trusted. But who was she? If only he could contact her.

Then, as his fatigue took hold, he stretched out on the bed, and switched out the light. He was tired too.

***

The orangey neon light filtered through the sky light and cast a luminous screen on the opposite wall, just as it had all those months before, though this time the freezing fog outside made the bough of the tree appear all blurred. It no longer swayed for now it was still and dead in the night. He turned on his side, to the empty half of the bed and groaned.

But then a movement from the corner of his eye made him face the neon screen on the wall again. There was no wind, so why had the bough moved?

No – not the bough – a shadow –

Suddenly he turned towards the door of the room as someone, or something – a presence – moved towards him. Startled, he sat upright and banged his head against the wall. He gasped and fumbled for the light switch. Instinctively, he covered his face with his arm in defence as the light blinded him – there – a woman – with the long ringlets of hair... again. But its shape, so curvaceous and perfectly formed, what ever it was, stood before him still and cold like that of a stone.

Eventually he lowered his guard. His fear dissipated as he became transfixed at what he saw. She had curls and plaits of hair twisted into ringlets almost down to her waist, and she was dressed in a black cat suit, which amply displayed her figure. She stood self-assured and with an air of coolness, as if to prove her dominance over anyone who happened to be in her presence. Barely conscious of his actions, he looked back at the photograph of the stone circle on the wall, as he recalled the half forgotten, fuzzy image of the woman that he thought he saw the night he spent with Emma. He looked back at the woman in front of him. She smiled, but it was neither warm nor welcoming, more a passive and emotionless smile of superiority, and her lips remained closed. It unnerved him. The skin of her face and neckline seemed ivory smooth and pale, in spite of the lamplight, and she just stared at him, as though her eyes were taking in his every thought, his every weakness and his every fear from way back.

"Who are you? How did you get in?"

The cold smile broadened as she raised her hand and jangled a set of keys in front of her.

"I arrived here before you. I have been here with you ever since you arrived. I can be invisible to you."

Her voice, though articulate, seemed odd - alien almost. Her speech was broken, so English was definitely not her native tongue.

"Not possible." He felt rather stupid, and as she glanced towards the picture he did the same. She was teasing him and not in a nice way, and he was confused.

"I am Megan. I befriended Emma. She was kind. I enjoyed her presence. It was good to be with another female entity. We talked. We both had an interest in the ring of stones. She worked for Forrester. I work for Forrester also… that is Forrester thinks I work for him, just like the little man called Hobson who runs the hotel thinks he can own me too.

"You are Sam, I know this. You were the new male in Emma's life were you not?"

She was going too fast for him; it was unnatural and he wanted her to slow down.

"Well I...What? You keep on talking of Emma in the past tense!" Alarm bells in his head were now adding to Sam's confusion.

She ignored him.

"Apart from her keys, the fragments of diary were all that I could salvage before they took her. I posted the few pages I saved here. I reasoned that you would come here also. Yes?"

He looked involuntarily at the manila envelope again. He hadn't noticed before; Emma's address was written on it, but it was addressed to him.

"Took her? Where? What do you mean? What have they done?"

She leant forward and placed her finger on his lips to quieten him.

"You know, you should learn to relax Sam. Live for now; not for past; not for future. When you have seen all that I have seen..."

"But you're so young – "

"Not so."

She had one of those faces; youthful but with a look in her eyes that betrayed a whole lifetime of wisdom and experience.

"Many lifetimes over." She was reading his thoughts. "Think about it…when I last saw you?"

"But" –

"Oh yes…after the night you last saw Carter; the circle of stone in your dreams as you call them? I was in communion with the stones and the lost souls trapped inside them over the millennia. They are just like me – though I return here over and over – many lifetimes in this form you keep seeing."

"You're completely mad."

But he did remember – the mysterious spectre that performed the eerie ritual, when the bronze ring went missing.

She was unperturbed. "In this form, I escape from stone, then they... *he* kill me again, over and over… the night of the metal men you call soldiers, so painful… and maybe he kill me in future also."

In spite of it all, it seemed to make sense, here in the dead of night, and in her presence.

"Ah, and the girl on the posters, on every tree. Of course…"

"No. I know nothing of that. But you recognise me, Sam Layton, ever since you were small boy…you saw me at top of tower, in your visions; that is your power, you see souls existing through great expanses of time."

Her body was close to him, and he could feel her breath. What kind of power she had over him, he couldn't fathom, but it quietened him. He felt peculiarly calm, in spite of the desperation he felt inside.

She knelt on the bed beside him. Next thing he knew she had unzipped the cat suit to her waist and was peeling off her t-shirt.

"What the hell are you doing?"

"I think I should stay here the night with you and discuss our search for Emma and her fate in the morning." She completed her disrobement and her pale naked form knelt beside him.

"And also, I would like to experience what she has experienced; the warmth of her flesh, and now of your flesh. So warm, like blood… and heartbeats. Not pain and cold of stone and swords, but warm delights of flesh."

For a moment – just a brief moment, he was about to surrender to her exquisite intoxication but, as she climbed under the duvet, a feeling of disgust welled up within him.

"No! This is wrong… you're crazy and I don't trust you!"

At last her self-assured smile dropped and her expression became quite serious.

"Very well, but remember I am your only friend… just like I was Emma's only friend. Yes? And what else have you to go on? Scrap of diary! And anyway, you have your own demons yes? You know that but I will help you."

How could she have known that? How did she know so much about him?

She stepped out of the bed and as she covered her ivory smooth contours of flesh, part of him regretted his last decision.

On her way to the door, she turned and said, "Be ready by two o'clock tomorrow afternoon. I shall be waiting for you in a Land Rover on the road outside this apartment. Be there."

When he heard the outer door click shut he took stock of the situation. Megan was right; apart from the diary or a visit to the Daughters of Carrawburgh stone circle itself, she was his only lead. He would just have to trust her.

When he turned out the lamp, dark thoughts closed in on him. Emma was dead, in which case it *was* her spirit that he saw in the churchyard.

14

The following morning passed interminably and was made worse by the fact that he never left the apartment. But sure enough, at two o'clock prompt, the noise of an engine's motor rumbled from the street below as it came to a halt. He peered out from the tiny window, and with butterflies in his stomach he descended the hall stairs. By the time he entered the street, the passenger door was already open. In her customary broken English and matter of fact manner, she said, "I will drive you to the circle of stone. It is the only way. You know that."

Then she simply stared ahead with her hands on the steering wheel.

A freezing grey fog had descended over the landscape so, as they drove into the fells, he could not see any further than a few yards ahead of the truck. The headlights peered into an empty void and there was nothing to guide them, save for the cats' eyes as the road twisted and curved. His eyes focussed on them and his mind drifted away until, eventually, she broke the silence, "You are like the priests who lived when the circle was young. You have the power to contact the ones whose life cycles are over, Emma told me so."

"If you mean I have the *gift*, not the power to get in touch with the departed, then yes I do." Sam begrudged her intrusive remark. "And it's hard for me to take in the fact that the dramas, and the pain and the hopes of these people occurred thousands of years ago. To me, they're still warm and vibrant in my mind."

"So think about the priest Cernunnos. He talked of how his people believed that the sacred stones absorbed the souls of the dead like a sponge of psychic energy, and how the priests were able to communicate with them... to tap into that power. If Emma's life cycle has been terminated early, then at the circle you will be able to recognise her spirit, and distinguish it quite clearly from all the dead souls lost over the eons… they will not be familiar to you."

He was astonished at her insensitivity. It was the way she spoke of things in such a cold manner – the way she used such phrases as 'life cycle terminated'.

"You talk so strangely… almost as if you are not human. You are as cold as stone."

He noticed a rueful smile appear on her lips. "You must love her. I know this. I offered myself to you in the night but you declined. Bodies are warm, stones are cold… when you are trapped in them for eternity… but no matter."

He did not understand and he tried to make sense of what she said, and of the crazy conversation they'd had late last night. She was deranged.

The stillness of the ice-cold greyness of his surrounds threatened to envelop and overwhelm him, as did his feeling of isolation and solitude. He turned his head and looked at his eerie companion. There were no winter clothes to cover her. She never shivered, nor did she make the slightest movement unless spoken to. And her eyes… always studying, always absorbing information. The light, feeble though it was, never shone or cast a shadow on her – it just bypassed her as if she did not belong in their surroundings. It made him feel uneasy. It was as though she wasn't real, just a figment of his mind.

It was just the same as his encounter with Forrester on the night of his visit. Indeed they were alike in some ways. Both had talked about the souls of the dead being trapped inside the megaliths and both talked about communicating with them through psychic means. Was it possible? He thought back to the nightmares he had as an infant and the voices from the stones as they whispered to him. Then he thought of the Roman soldier Arrian and his horrific account of the sacrifice, and the figure of a woman with ringlets and plaits of hair as she emerged from behind a megalith and fled into the darkness. Then he looked at the figure seated beside him again.

He shivered, more through his growing unease than from the cold.

As she drove, an outline of a small building formed out of the mist and murk ahead. He assumed that it was an old coaching inn, and it probably dated back from several centuries ago. She pulled up beside it and stepped out. He followed.

A rusty mist soaked sign hung by a small parking

bay. It simply said 'Inn: no vacancies in winter' and below it: 'Druid's circle one mile', but Sam was already walking over to the small car in the corner, which stood frozen and neglected. It was Emma's – so she never even made it away from the inn. A lump formed in his throat.

He noticed the dull yellow glow of tungsten light through the window of the building and his first instinct was to confront the occupants, but Megan barred his way.

"No time!" she asserted in her broken English. "We must make our way to circle on foot. Come now!"

He followed her brief glance towards the limousine at the other end of the tarmac but she was already striding ahead and disappearing into the fog.

They left the road and walked across the grass and gorse. The coldness and damp seeped through his boots and it was difficult to keep up with her pace but, as the ground rose, a pale watery sun attempted to break through the mist. As it grew stronger, it bathed the grass and scrub in an opaque light green colour, though its iridescence failed to show on the dark and shapely form striding ahead of him.

"We walk up to the crest of hill, and as we approach, Daughters of Carrawburgh stone circle will appear. The land will then be familiar to you from your first visit."

True to her word, as they reached the top of the rise the nearest megalith poked above the horizon. When they arrived they simply stopped and surveyed the scene. It was just as Emma had described – the ancient stones, too many to count, stood there silently, waiting for the spiritual, the unsuspecting, and the foolhardy to visit them. The ancient oak stood proud and imposing at the centre, and beyond were the three foothills. This was the land and how Arrian saw it nearly two thousand years before, and the clan of people who worshipped the stones thousands of years before his time.

"Emma said that one stone was missing, but I can't see where," he said.

"No, even you won't see the gap. Most are unaware that one remains missing."

Without waiting for a reply, she headed off for the nearest stone with the same rapid and purposeful stride. Sam looked on. She stopped and placed her hands upon it, and appeared to stare into it with great intensity. Though just like before in his dream, it was one of the strangest things he had ever seen. She was actually trying to read it – to communicate with it in some way. She moved her hands along the column from time to time, and then she crouched, stood up, and embraced it. This went on for several minutes, but then she abruptly broke away and moved on to the next stone and repeated the process, before moving on to a third.

By now the sun had broken through and the whole area was cast in bright winter sunlight, yet the moving black figure that was Megan still reflected no light, and appeared unreal, ghostly even.

But he reminded himself of the urgency of the situation. He crossed the embankment and entered the circle. He walked among the stones aimlessly, he was simply putting his trust and faith in any recently departed souls who wished to contact him. That was his way. They both performed their psychic ritual apart from one another, in silence and in their own way.

But the images and shapes of the stones took a hold, and before long one stone in particular caught his eye. His heart missed a beat when he recognised it. It was the one from his nightmare – the night Emma had visited him in his dream – the night she sank beneath the stone – dead. He walked and then ran towards it as his mind raced ahead of him. He fell to his knees before it as its overbearing form loomed over him, and he felt her presence in an instant – warm and vivid. His worst fears were unfolding before him. A tightness gripped at his chest when he noticed the freshly dug earth at the base of the ancient stone. So this was where her life had ended; this was where she lay – cold, alone and neglected – and for what purpose? Why had he not been there for her?

He clawed at the disturbed earth with his bare hands. In his increasing despair, he had no time to think about the figure standing beside him – that is, until she spoke, "Stop. You must stop this and wait." The voice of Megan made him stop abruptly. Still on his knees, he looked up at the perfect form of the woman standing over him. As always, she continued to study him, then her eyes turned their attention to his torn and bloody fingers. He was compelled to do so as well, and he stared at his hands. It made him realise how pathetic he must have appeared. His attention returned to her eyes once more.

She stretched out her hand and helped him to his feet.

"Trust me... through the approaching darkness, trust me."

At that moment the watery sun, ever low in the sky, passed behind a megalith and cast the terrain in shadow. Already the early evening of winter approached. The sound of voices drifted over from the huge portal stones at the eastern entrance. Three figures were emerging from the gloom but he instantly recognised the tallest: the unmistakable swagger of Forrester, still attired in the dark trench coat, and still with an elegant glove wrapped around the handle of his ebony cane.

"Stay here," she commanded and she walked briskly over to them.

Sam watched on helplessly whilst a long and unheard discussion took place between the distant figures. Then Forrester, with his cool arrogance, gestured with his forefinger for him to approach. Megan nodded at Sam as if to reassure him.

"Ah Layton old chap, I offer my congratulations. I understand that you have found Mrs. Carter and she is exactly where I had hoped."

His cold, malignant smile confirmed his worst nightmare, but before he had time to react, Megan linked her arm around Forrester's.

"I'm sorry Sam, really I am," she said, "but we

needed a sacrifice, an offering, in order to complete the circle."

Her tone seemed remorseful, yet it was difficult to take in this latest twist; "Trust me," she had said. He had been totally duped and fooled, and felt so wretched.

"And now it *is* complete… and with only a matter of hours to go," Forrester added, his smugness never wavering. A frown appeared momentarily on his aristocratic brow as he continued:

"Quite appropriate really don't you think? I employ her for her skills in the field of science and so forth, and then I use her to complete the rituals; the last sacrifice. She should actually feel quite honoured, so it's a shame she's not here to appreciate it. Well, I couldn't let her go, so I was just getting the most from her… recycling my resources you might say!"

The smile broadened as he patted the hand of Megan, still linked around his arm.

"Of course it was the fair lady Morrigan here that executed the distasteful deed, though I think she calls herself Megan now. Well it's more realistic isn't it in this modern and materialistic age, no gods and goddesses anymore…

"Yes, she gained our widow's trust just as she did yours, but you see I've survived through the ages by trusting no one. I conjured up this little ruse for her to lure you here, and thus, in one neat trick, she's proven her loyalty to me and got you to confirm that she has indeed used the woman as a sacrifice. You're the only person who knows of her disappearance of course, so it's good to know you're here where I want you."

Forrester looked at Megan, who still wore that dreadful impassive smile, and patted her hand again.

"Yes, all very neat I think."

Sam shook his head uselessly, "Just who the hell are you both?"

Megan's smile dropped and her studious eyes seemed cold and unforgiving.

"I am Morrigan, or call me Megan or what you will; I am ageless. I am retribution. I am the dark side of your thoughts, in lust and in violence. You lust for me Sam, do you not? I am not evil, but I am a vengeful spirit - you know that - you felt the soldier Arrian's fate. He had betrayed my people and was responsible for our sister Brigit's death."

"Yes all very fanciful I'm sure," Forrester interrupted. "It's impossible to fully understand, even for us, but we are the sum parts of all the dead spirits and their psychic energy absorbed into this stone temple through the ages. There is so much psychic energy here, layer upon layer, so that it's formed a force - no, a *life* of its own. Your Neolithic ancestors understood. We simply take on physical form every two thousand years or so."

For a moment the arrogance faded, and his speech became vague, "Not sure why… something to do with the alignment of the stars to the megaliths…the three stars in the belt of Orion and those hills yonder. But for centuries in between, my spirit, or whatever I am, lies dormant on that hill you call Cragburn… then they built that house..."

A frown appeared across the aristocrat's eyebrows as the light shone onto his forehead and dark, greying hair. Unexpectedly, he appeared hesitant and confused.

"I remember a man taking residence there… a learned man… his mind was so powerful. He took an interest in the sciences, and of the culture and beliefs of our ancestors. I can recall a whole library of books, ranging from subjects as diverse as astronomy, mathematics, and of the dark arts… and then there were his collections of artifacts and antiquities.

"Once it had been easy to inhabit the minds and bodies of mortals like the priests and shamans such as Cernonnus who believed in the power of the dead. Now, the opportunity arose again, in the body of Edward Forrester… the story of the recluse taking up residence in the house on Carrawburgh fells and being driven insane by solitude is well documented."

Then, his confidence and demeanor returned as swiftly as it had gone.

"You know all of this Layton, you could sense mine and Morrigan's presence as an infant. I need to talk to you about that," his tone had become softer, "which is why I want you to stay as our guest at the inn tonight."

A desperate feeling of isolation and fear gripped Sam when he realised that he was alone with two malevolent spirits in a landscape that was miles away from anyone living.

With a gesture of his gloved hand, the two henchmen hovering behind then closed in on Sam.

"My colleagues Messrs Hobson and Gunter will escort you back where you will wait. I will join you shortly."

He turned swiftly and moved as though heading for the great oak at the centre.

"See you later old chap!" he called, with his back turned away from Sam.

The air had already chilled as the late afternoon sun began to fade. Darkness would soon take a hold, just as it had already done in Sam's heart.

15

Like a prisoner under guard, Sam was almost frog-marched into the tiny foyer of the inn. It was no more than a tiny hallway with a shabby, wooden-panelled reception desk, behind which a curtain hid what Sam assumed to be a small office. A narrow stairway led off from the right and an archway on the opposite side led to the bar.

Hobson went over to the opposite side of the desk and fidgeted as he turned the visitors' book towards Sam.

"Surely you don't expect me to sign the visitors' book. That's preposterous."

"So's we've a record of you being here... just in case we're found out."

"Yeah, you know the headline: 'Woman found dead in kinky ritual, boyfriend, chief suspect, goes berserk and kills 'er'," added Gunter with a crooked grin.

Hobson shuffled his feet uneasily and wiped the beads of perspiration from his brow betraying his unease.

"OK Gunter, I'll handle this. Mr Forrester says we've got to go easy on him." But the smirk never left Gunter's face as he disappeared through the archway to the bar.

"Don't even think you're going anywhere," Hobson added, "he's only gone for a drink and a ciggy, and you wouldn't want to upset him."

But Sam was beaten, and he simply looked down on the reception desk.

"Look mate," Hobson whispered and leant forward as though he wanted to confess something and rid himself of guilt, "I never wanted any of this but, well, you know what Forrester's like, he lends you money, takes your business, and before you know it, you're under his spell, well…"

He reached for a key from a series of hooks on the wall behind him.

"You can stay in her room…your girlfriend's; it's the only decent room in the inn. Go on, get up them stairs."

Wearily Sam climbed the stairs, but Hobson was close behind him, as though anxious not to lose his master's prize. He ushered him through the first door into a tiny bedroom and caught Sam's glance at the forced lock on the door and instantly read Sam's thought. His sweating and fidgeting increased.

"Look, I don't know what happened to her that evening, so don't blame me. Gunter and that tart, what's her name, Megan, took her off. I didn't take to her… she's just a prick tease, just a reception girl with an attitude. Personally, I wish they'd all just clear out… trouble the lot of 'em. All I want is to go back to running my hotel – I wanted none of this. Just don't you go giving me any hassle; if you're thinking of going anywhere, Gunter will be only too happy to keep you in the bar, and he aint friendly!"

With that, he shut the door and disappeared, leaving

Sam with nothing, except time to think and brood.

He sat on the bed and held his head in his hands. Now alone, his despair began to take hold. Poor Emma! Cold, alone, and with her fate sealed in that desolate place on the fells. His tortured mind speculated over what her final moments… her final *thoughts* must have been like and then the horrors of what Arrian saw on the night of the sacrifice during his time on the earth flooded back to him. It made it unbearable.

But he shook his head; he had to keep going and to find some inner strength within him, not for his own sake but for hers. He had to bring the perpetrators to justice. If only he could get away and buy just a little time so as to alert the authorities. No matter how fantastic his story, the authorities were bound to take notice because there were just too many deaths – first the girl on the poster, then Paul and now his widow. The local police couldn't be all be under Forrester's control. He cursed for allowing himself to be tricked by the obvious charms of Megan – using the oldest and most basic ploy – in luring him there.

With a sense of hopelessness, his eyes searched the room looking for clues – anything in his search for another scrap of information. Maybe there was something of Emma's left behind which would tell the story of her final hours. He searched the wardrobe, the chest of drawers and under the bed – perhaps something was accidentally left behind when she was hurriedly abducted from the room. Nothing materialised.

Suddenly the thought occurred to him that there might be further fragments of diary hidden away. Quickly he crossed over to the tiny bureau by the window, and pulled open the drawer:

Keys – Emma's car keys! What a thing for them to overlook! *"Fools!"* he triumphed.

He looked out of the window that overlooked the road. The car, unmistakeably hers, was still parked in the lay-by opposite, all neglected and coated with frost and dew.

The door, driven by a chilly drought, had creaked open and it was now a few inches ajar. Of course! The lock had been broken, no doubt as a result of her struggle and eventual doom, but now it could turn out to be his salvation.

A series of opportunities were now presented to him, but there was no time to formulate a plan or talk himself out of it. This would probably be his one and only chance. Yet he remained hesitant – even if he did make it to the car it was cold and misted over, so that even if it did start, he wouldn't be able to see where he was going, and by that time Gunter and Hobson would be on top of him. Frantically, his mind raced for another option but there was nothing, and anyway, they wouldn't dare kill him, as Forrester had commanded it so. They would just make it painful for him that's all.

He looked out of the window again. The light was fading. The pale, watery sun had given up, and the grey, damp mist of the freezing fog was taking over once more

– so typical of the Northumbrian fells. It was now or never.

Quietly, he stepped onto the landing, but he had barely taken two steps when Gunter, who stood at the bottom of the stairs, confronted him. For a split second they froze as their eyes met, until the crooked smirk appeared on Gunter's lips. It was clear he was aching for a fight. Just the sight of his bulky frame and the bull-neck and shaven head had put paid to Sam's plans.

Then, the thug began to climb the stairs. Sam backed away and sighed, but then a flash of inspiration hit him, seemingly from nowhere. For a moment, a split second in time, Gunter would be vulnerable… Sam pressed down his hands onto the banister either side of him, hoisted himself upwards and thrust out with both legs forward, kicking Gunter in the midriff. With an oafish grunt, he went crashing down the stairs, until he hit the back of his head against the wall where the steps veered around in a curve. Sam raced down the stairs and tried to pass him, but Gunter grabbed his ankle as he went by. As Sam toppled over, his hand instinctively grabbed at a picture frame, dislodging it from the wall. It crashed down onto Gunter's face. Sam fell onto him and as a disorientated Gunter's arms flayed helplessly, he pressed his hand on the back of the frame and onto his enemy's face until he heard the glass crack. As Gunter squealed, Sam's heart pounded, as hate welled up from within him.

"And that's from Emma!" he spat as he continued to press hard.

He had but a moment to take in the irony of the water colour picture as it came free of the frame – it was of the stone circle – when a shout came from behind him:

"Oi, you can't leave, Forrester wants you!"

It was Hobson. For a second, Sam just looked at him. He was as frightened as he was, and he realised this overweight, sweaty man was just as hesitant, Swiftly, Sam pushed him aside, just as Gunter groaned and began to stir back to consciousness.

He ran into the yard, and straight across the thankfully deserted road. Frantically, he fumbled for the car keys. His heart thumped and thumped and his hands just wouldn't stop shaking. Any second now, he expected hands to grab him by the collar. After what seemed like an eternity, the door opened and he fell into the driver's seat.

"Please, please start, damn you!"

The engine failed. He punched the steering wheel with his fists.

"Slowly…slowly." He tried to calm himself. Then, on the third attempt, it fired. His foot pressed clumsily down on the accelerator, making the engine screech into life. Hobson was but a few feet away. He slammed the car into gear and released the clutch. The car jolted and lurched, but miraculously it never stalled. It moved away with a screech from the tyres just as Hobson put his hand on the door, but it was too late for him to get any purchase on it.

"I can't see…I can't see!" Sam shouted uselessly and

to no-one but himself. The car spun and somehow must have turned right around. More in panic than by design, Sam pressed the accelerator to the floor making the engine roar again. Then, as the car shot forward, there was a horrid and loud thud in front somewhere, and a cracking sound like the splintering of wood and then a scream – this time human, all in a split second.

No, not wood, it was bone!

Hobson landed face down on the bonnet, with his face pressed to the outside of the windscreen. The frozen and grotesque, wide-eyed stare of a dead man with blood oozing from an open mouth was but a few inches away from Sam as he let out his own cry of anguish.

Instinctively, he shut his eyes and jerked the steering wheel rapidly from side to side, just to get the image of that awful staring face out of his vision. Sure enough, the body fell away and disappeared into the foggy grey murk.

Somehow, he held onto the last vestiges of coherent thought as he switched on the windscreen wipers and headlights and drove. He knew he was all over the road and could barely see a few feet ahead as the windscreen refused to defrost. How fortunate it was that this was such a lonely stretch of road and in the middle of nowhere.

After a short while, when his panic stricken mind calmed and the pounding of his heart had subsided, he slowly drew the car to a halt. The engine still ticked over and only very gradually did he release his iron grip of the steering wheel. But he dare not step out and away from the sanctuary of the car. Exhausted, he let his head fall backwards onto the headrest and exhaled.

16

Night had fallen when Sam turned the key in the door of Emma's apartment. By the time he had brought her car to a halt outside in the street below, the cold and wet mist had returned and it mingled with the neon glow, muffling out any sounds of the night. All was silent and still. The horrors of the day had left him like a stunned and wounded animal, wandering aimlessly around with no particular purpose. He had nowhere else to go.

The first thing he noticed was the lamp switched on in the living room. Megan sat astride the sofa with her feet upon the armrest and her arms folded. It had come as little surprise to Sam to find her waiting for him. Although all the fight and adrenalin had been drained from him, he still resented the way she had made the place her own. The darkness of her catsuit appeared charcoal grey and blended into the dimly lit surroundings. There seemed to be a curious diffuse and pale shade of light surrounding her so that she appeared almost like a hologram - more so as her pale skin seemed almost iridescent as it glowed in the light. The curves of her flesh were perfection, and a repellent mixture of loathing and physical desire for her welled up within him.

"Like the proverbial cuckoo in the nest; make yourself comfortable why don't you?" he muttered to himself as he walked over to the opposite chair and flopped down.

"Trust me through the encroaching darkness," she repeated with the customary impassive smile so that it was difficult to tell whether she was mocking him or not.

Although he was long since past any fear, he detected a movement from the corner of his eye coming from the shadows near the bookcase and it made him start. Another dark and semi-formed patch of darkness lurked from within.

Forrester emerged from the gloom. At first all Sam saw was the reflection of the lamplight in a pair of dark eyes and then, a split second later, the form of his tall frame and black trench coat materialised, seemingly out of thin air. How could Sam have failed to notice his presence the moment he walked into the apartment?

"I knew you would get the better of my underlings," he said, in a quieter tone than Sam was accustomed to, "and in a way I'm pleased."

"You won't be," Sam hissed, "especially when I go to the police."

Megan moved her legs from the armrest, allowing Forrester to sit beside her.

"You won't do that," Forrester smiled confidently, "you still don't appreciate the extent of my domain do you?"

"Oh, but they'll listen! Anything associated with the circle… the murdered girl last summer, the death of Paul Carter…"

"She was unimportant... a nobody, and merely a component in a failed experiment. I wanted her soul as the final link to complete the psychic ring, the last sacrificial victim. But it failed, her bloodline and ancestry failed to connect. It seems that she was not of my blood and semen after all. Her mother had lied to me...betrayed me. She paid the price. Of course it made the sacrifice of her daughter easier to bear but, as she had no bloodline to our original clan, I was a fool to think it would work."

"And that's how you see it all, as an experiment? Well it disgusts me."

"I'm not the first to try Sam. You saw the victim at Edwulf's tower – the one that Carter disturbed, bricked up from centuries ago. Not just the bones of course, but you also witnessed her restless spirit. You noticed how she was adorned with the long plaits and ringlets of hair and the bronze ring? The fools were trying to ape our ancestors."

"And what of Paul? I knew it couldn't have been an accident."

"Carter was an arrogant upstart." Forrester's brutal posturing returned for a moment. "He stole what was mine – the bronze rings, so necessary for the sacrifices, so he paid the price, and in return I took what was his – his wife to complete the work and the experiment."

Sam tried to control the rage welling up within him, but then Megan leaned forward and placed her hand on his shoulder, "No matter, her soul has joined the dead along with all my sisters."

"Oh, and did all this involve your pathetic act of changing the girl and my Emma's hair to resemble yours Megan? And the wearing of the bronze ring?" Sam bit his lip. "Was this done before or after you had killed them?"

"Girl yes, Emma no."

"Enough, all this is irrelevant!" Forrester raised his leather-gloved palm so as to put an end to the exchange. "Emma Carter was far more suitable, and has been most useful."

Sam lunged forward but Forrester never flinched. Instead, the silver-tipped cane held in his other hand, came forward and formed a barrier.

"Sam you must calm down," he said but there was no longer malevolence in his voice, and his condescending manner had vanished. "You won't go to the authorities, and you will soon forget her...I guarantee it after what I am about to tell you."

"Emma was my sister in death," Megan intervened as if to try and comfort Sam. "But she was just flesh and blood, soft and warm but ephemeral, soon to wither, age and decay, and then be forgotten. But now she is serving some greater purpose."

"Emma was not like us, but not like you either," Forrester continued.

"What?" Sam hissed again as he fidgeted and rubbed the back of his neck with his palm.

Forrester hesitated for a moment, an unusual occurrence. He seemed not to know how to explain his next revelation.

"You must remember me from when you were an infant…when I visited and spoke to your mother on several occasions, and you watched from your play pen in the other room? You saw us talking about things your young mind couldn't possibly understand."

Sam nodded agitated. "The man in the dark coat… oh yes, but I suppose I never wanted to admit to myself that I recognised you, that is until you crossed me at Edwulf's tower. 'Just like your mother' – you used those words when you confronted us. Then I knew!"

"Precisely – just like your mother. I passed on the psychic power that you possess through her, so you're *like* me."

"Not like you… not like you…" Sam shook his head. "Besides are you saying she had the gift as well? Because that can't be, no, she didn't understand my visions and nightmares, she –"

"No Sam, that's not what I'm saying. *I* passed on the gift, or the power, call it what you will…"

The penny dropped and Sam felt himself redden and his jaw drop.

"That's right Sam. You're my flesh and blood…my gene pool. You are one of us."

Sam lunged at him again, and this time his hand made contact around Forrester's throat, but there was no strength and no will; it dissipated the moment he found himself staring into the man's dark and impassive eyes, like looking into an abyss.

Effortlessly, the gloved hand took hold of Sam's and

pushed it away. Forrester remained unmoved and chillingly calm, and once again, Sam slipped back into his chair.

For a moment all three remained silent. Sam calmed himself, and then quietly spoke again, "What happened to my mother?"

Forrester looked at his hands again in that way Sam had noticed. He unbuttoned the gloves and studied his long fingers in his curious way.

"She's well I expect. She's far away, and has started a new life. It's possible she has a new family. Sam, you have to understand that I have sired many offspring in order to carry on the original clan's bloodline, with various females I deemed suitable, until I was able to produce an heir with the same powers – you. But all of them, though far away, enjoy my protection. I would never harm them…"

Sam was having difficulty coming to terms with it all. Megan knew, and intervened again in an attempt to move on to other matters:

"Tell him about tomorrow... tell him about alignment of stars."

Forrester paused, and then began, "Do you remember when I asked you to consider what it must be like to contact and commune with the dead from long ago? Think of the knowledge and the wisdom you could attain. And with knowledge and wisdom, comes *power!* That's just what our ancestors did, and even though I don't really understand why, I was *there*… thousands of years ago…when they built their barrow on the fells. The priests handed their knowledge down from generation to generation… I *was* one of the priests. When the spirits of their dead became too numerous to count, they built the circle of stone, a ring of magic if you like, so as to keep all that psychic energy concentrated in one small area of sacred earth. Don't you see? They were trying to keep the spirits *in*, not intruders out, which is the popular belief held today. That's what is so unique about this henge…the barrow, and the human sacrifices at each of the stones – all that concentrated psychic energy – it's all still intact. That's the reason I needed Mrs. Carter's expertise – so that she could confirm this fact… well one of the reasons I needed her anyway. She has, or let's say her spirit has, a bond with you. And as you are of my bloodline, that bond extends to me. I had no such bond with my imposter daughter Fleur, hence she was unsuitable.

"Tomorrow, you will see how the three stars, the ones you call the belt of Orion, rise in exact alignment with the three distant hills – the land where our ancestors begin their journey to the next world… it happens every two thousand years. My consciousness awakens and I find my self born into another body… the priest-shaman Cernunnos… now Forrester… and it is only at the point of this two thousand year cycle, that I can awaken the power of the spirits. Four thousand years ago, when the stones were brought here, they began their life… two thousand years ago when the Romans came, and just like you, they misunderstood and they cut me down. But here I am again as I wait for events to unfold..."

Forrester had completed his fantastic statement with such calmness and authority, Sam was drawn in.

With that, he rose from the chair, replaced his gloves and picked up his cane. It was only then that Sam had noticed that Megan was already standing in the doorway waiting for Forrester, her fecund shape silhouetted against the hall light. Once again her silent and invisible movement appeared unnatural. And a spasm of longing shot through him again, as well as jealousy at the thought of Forrester's ownership of her.

Forrester turned to Sam once more before he walked towards her, "The missing Alnilam stone… there was a gap, so through Emma's sacrifice the psychic ring is complete again. You will be at the circle of stone after dark tomorrow, I know."

17

The stars shone from a crisp and clear winter sky and Sam thought how different things looked now. Just a few hours earlier the ring of stones, silent and still, slept in the cold dank air, but now that darkness had fallen they had awoken. They glowed as they shimmered blood red from the heat of the flames.

A moment ago he had stood and looked down from the ridge above – the very same place he had first met Emma all that time ago. Now, here he was again, demanding answers to questions the man Forrester had imposed on his very life and soul.

He had watched in awe as the oak at its centre had been set ablaze by a figure cloaked in a long white shroud, whose face was hidden by a mask. Maybe it was due to the fading light, but it seemed to have appeared out of the darkness from nowhere, and now stood inert as it waited for the flames to grow and take hold, and so consume the trunk and boughs of the mighty tree.

But then the figure turned and looked at him with its eerie, manikin-like stare. Sam stood transfixed, caught in the shaman's gaze. Then it gestured with an outstretched arm for Sam to approach. Whether it was a subjugation of his will or a simple morbid desire to end all of his suffering, Sam wasn't sure, but as he descended he almost welcomed the warmth coming from the flames as it dissipated the chill of the night.

As he drew nearer, the strange figure unveiled its mask. He recognised the face staring at him in the red glow from the flames – Forrester – though now the suit and tie had been replaced by the ceremonial gown, and instead of the elegant cane he held a human tibia. In the other hand he clasped the skull, no doubt belonging to the bone's long dead owner. A sword, rested on the buckle of the man's belt. Any trace of the self-assured smile had vanished, and instead, amidst the fiery glow of the flames, there was a distinct crazed look in his eyes and face.

But, for a moment, the man who was once the unflappable persona of Forrester seemed to emerge again from behind the possessed being, as he spoke, "Before you say anything Sam Layton, you will desist from calling me a druid – it's tiresome and I am nothing of the sort, well, not in the sense that you mean. No, I am not about to involve myself in some hippy style, pot smoking fest, nor am I using the term in vain as our Victorian forbears did as they sated their frustrations by indulging in some middle-aged sexual orgy. No, I prefer to call myself a keeper of knowledge. Have you any idea what I am talking about Sam? Have you?"

"I know you've taken away from me everything I hold dear… my mother, Emma, and even my calling… my spirituality, my gift; all of it beholden to you… all of these existed because of you. *I* exist because of you."

"It's all irrelevant my dear Sam, just flesh and blood – temporary, ephemeral as I've said before – it withers, dies and decays. Tomorrow, your dramas and your cares will be forgotten... blown away with the wind, and eroded by time."

He turned to stand aside Sam and looked into the night sky, and then pointed with the long bone:

"Look at that!" His dark eyes glistened red by the light of the flames.

The three stars that formed the belt of Orion had risen, and appeared to rest on the darkened outlines of the three foothills to the northeast.

"An optical illusion, nothing more."

"Come now, that's not like you, don't be so morose," Forrester retorted. "It's the exact alignment that only happens every two thousand years that's so important. They wouldn't have understood – my clan...*your* clan. They thought our spirits travelled from the stones where their bodies were consecrated, into the underworld that existed under those hills, guided by three pin-pricks of light that shone in the sky. Well... they could see the hills, they were tangible; they could walk there and touch them. Every time they gazed at their own image, cast by the reflection in the rivers and streams, they believed they were looking through a window to that underground domain, and that the spirits that dwelt there had captured their soul... a blueprint for when they eventually joined them there. They couldn't possibly have understood about the universe, and the vast distances of other worlds and of the nature of starlight."

"Are you trying to tell me that our spirit energy, once it's left our mortal bodies, travels to the stars… those stars?"

"Well why not? It's a theory, nothing more… of course it is. We know little more than our ancestors, that's why I have to communicate with them. Come on Layton, you and your brethren are the first to believe that when we die our essences move on to another existence, another plane… another world. Why not up there?" He jabbed the long bone into the sky. "Given the vast distances of the stars, it makes more sense than ever being able to travel there by starship doesn't it?"

In spite of everything, Sam found himself agreeing with him. He and his friends did believe in an afterlife, albeit undefined, but then he thought of the horrors he had been through.

"Yes, but my brethren as you call them, don't resort to ritual sacrifice and bloodlust."

But then Sam caught sight of a familiar figure as it entered the arena from the entrance on the far side. It was Gunter. His face, covered in fresh red scars and purple swollen bruises, bore a curious mixture of anger and a malevolent smirk, exaggerated by the glow of the flames. He was itching for revenge. Another burly individual followed him. It reminded Sam that he was still a prisoner, in spite of Forrester's attempts to win him round.

"I've told you," Forrester spat contemptuously, "flesh and blood is temporary. It's irrelevant. The bloodlust and the terror are necessary to generate and invoke or to *charge* the psychic energy. I needed one more female essence... one more soul in the ground near the missing stone, in order to complete the circle and harness the energy in a ring. The spirits that dwell dormant in the stones will awaken and give me knowledge, what I need to know."

Megan appeared somewhere from the stones on the other side of the flames. She was still dressed in her skin-tight black apparel and never flinched. She just stood there observing, not the scene before them but Forrester, as though she were assimilating every thought that lurked deep inside him.

"We live within the stones... inside of them. We *are* the stones. They are permanent, but they are hard and cold... unlike flesh. Come Cernunnos," she said, "it's time. Look at the stones."

All three turned their attention to the ring and became silent as they watched.

A thin patch of white mist began to form around each megalith. Though barely perceptible at first, they grew and they glided and swirled silently from stone to stone, just like will o' the wisps in the darkness. Then each one gradually began to take form and gain substance.

Ectoplasm! This was the first time Sam had seen it form before his very eyes, something he never thought he'd witness. The wisps became more concentrated and luminescent as they continued to swirl ever faster, seemingly with purpose as they gradually took shape and form. They moved from one stone to the next in an unearthly and silent dance.

"Use your powers man," Forrester was fired up. "See how the psychic energy forms before your eyes."

Overwhelmed, Sam backed against the fire at the centre. In spite of his inflated confidence, Forrester followed, "Look... look over there..."

More of the luminescent wisps were forming over on the far side of the ring, and followed the same sequence as they grew and darted from stone to stone. Just then, the flames from the fire blew away in a single moment and plunged them into darkness, save for a dull, red glow from the dying embers. The night air was still and silent, and now that the flames were doused, an icy chill penetrated Sam to the core.

From the burnt remains of the trunk and boughs of the oak, three headless skeletons now stood in a row; charred sticks of the dead, never allowed to rest. The blackened bones of their torsos were only just visible by the starlight and the embers of the dead fire.

Forrester became hesitant, not knowing what to do – a moment of indecision – but quickly followed by realisation displayed in a manic grin. Then a command it – pierced the eerie silence as he pointed towards them, "The founder of the Tribe...Mintaka, and his wives... Alnilam... Alnitak..."

Sam wanted to run, but his body remained rooted to the spot, frozen with cold and fear. Forrester showed no such reservations, and approached the nearest headless corpse in anticipation. He placed the skull he was nurturing on to the neck of the blackened, charred bones, and as the jaw dropped, the red glow from the pile of ash appeared through its eyes and mouth. A hideous grin of broken teeth from the long since dead stared back at them.

"Listen, listen now," Megan spoke, her voice as calm as ever.

Forrester and Sam strained their ears in dreadful anticipation. A cry, or perhaps a wail, broke the stillness of the night, and echoed among the stones. But the wail became more distinct and, like a banshee, grew louder until it sounded like a multitude of human voices, or screams. But these were not human voices – not any more anyway.

They looked above them. The luminous patches of mist were flying over their heads as well – in fact they were all around them now that the flames were extinguished and the darkness of night encroached. They continued on with their macabre dance, and their wailing cries – that of human anguish and despair – grew louder as they swirled and glided around them and through them, gaining speed and substance as they did so. They buffeted against Sam's body, like a hideous and unseen plague of insects, and they passed right through him, winding him and causing him to gasp. Now, they were forming into the shapes of human bodies – phantoms with hollows for eyes and mouths. And as they opened and closed, puffs of luminescent dust were belched out with each successive scream. He felt the particles spray onto his face.

Soon their movements and echoes reached to such a screaming pitch that they blurred into one. It seemed like one massive entity swirling around them, and with just one merged hollow shrill sounding in their ears. Its frantic pace and pitch continued to rise. The three of them just stood there bathed in the opaque mist as the phantoms danced around and through them in perfect equilibrium.

Sam was only vaguely aware of a deeper and more human cry from somewhere further out in the darkness. But he looked on in horror as a number of the phantoms wrapped around the bodies of Gunter and his sidekick with a rapidly increasing speed, like a viscous cyclone. Their bodies and limbs twitched as it tore them apart and the ectoplasmic shapes of light glowed with increasing intensity as though a kind of grisly hunger had become sated. One of them, he wasn't sure which, made a futile attempt to run towards the centre but the screaming phantoms engulfed him, just at the point where Sam was able to see the distorted face of the man melt away to the skull and then collapse into a pile of bones. It seemed that the ghastly entities could take life whenever they wanted, and any minute now…

"Their work is done," Forrester said, and he returned his manic gaze to the phantoms overhead. "See how the maidens dance in perfect harmony; the spirits of the dead are here... set free, and their powers are ready for me to harness."

As their own bodies glowed an eerie white from the spectres, the onlookers, all lost in their own thoughts, watched the dance of the dead. It showed no sign of ending. But then, quite abruptly, and for no apparent reason, the forms began to lose their integrity and dissolve. Quickly they collapsed, and the opaque mist drew itself back into the bodies of the megaliths at an incredible rate.

"What... what's happening?" Forrester's voice was wavering.

He stepped away from them and headed towards the perimeter. The others quickly followed.

He pointed towards the place where Emma's body had been interred. It remained shrouded in blackness and was untouched by the rapidly dissolving ectoplasm.

"The circle is not complete," he seethed between clenched teeth as his eyes narrowed.

Before anyone had a chance to respond he lashed out with his fist. Sam felt the sharp pain on his jaw and tasted the salty blood in his mouth. Then, the palm of Forrester's hand clamped tight as his fingers pressed around Sam's windpipe. The snarling mouth and the crazed eyes of the priest filled his already blurring vision.

"Damn you Layton, you've tricked me. What have you done? Tell me now!"

But then Forrester became hesitant and his grip loosened, making Sam topple to the ground. He clutched at his bruised throat, and rolled over as he gasped for air.

Forrester, his rage momentarily subdued, rubbed his chin in puzzlement, his calculating mind searching for an answer.

Sam took his chance – his anger and bitterness coiled like a tightened spring, he kicked out and struck Forrester on the shin. As he cried out, the priest crumpled, but Sam was on top of him. The palm and jeweled fingers aimed for Sam's throat again. This time, though, he was ready for him; he grabbed Forrester's wrist and their hate-filled eyes met. Sam knew his strength against the giant would fail. In desperation, he wrestled the long-bone still held in his opponent's other hand and released his grip on his other wrist. He swung the ancient tibia and hit him straight in the face with a swishing noise, like that of a cane.

Forrester screamed in pain, his strength lost as he rolled over, clutching his face. Blood flowed from his cheekbone and his mouth, which added to the manic glare from his darkened eyes.

"Stop this, stop this now." Megan stood over them both as they lay there on the ground, breathless and ebbed of strength. As always the expression on her face was impassive and untouched by the unfolding events.

"You were right to be wary of me Cernunnos for I have deceived you, and not Layton. The last time you were here, when the soldiers in their metal came and cut you to pieces with their blades, the psychic energy from the Alnilam stone which stood here, escaped. Its consciousness, born out of the souls of the many dead interred here, took human form… me. The soldier named Arrian witnessed it that night and described it to you Sam and I am truly sorry that I deceived you also." A rare look of compassion seemed to show in her eyes. "I had to lure you here in order to trick him into thinking that I was loyal to him. He has spies and henchmen everywhere."

Then she turned towards the priest again.

"Your arrogance born of the male kind, has caused you to make too many assumptions, yes? Just like you I am a sort of spirit born through the souls of the dead that dwell in the stones, but unlike you – you are a parasite, taking over priest mortals, and then soul of Edward Forrester – I am a conscious entity of the females that have been slain here. I am vengeful, I am retribution, but unlike you, I am not evil. As long as the living believe in me, no matter how few in numbers, then like you, I shall exist through eternity."

Anger and venom returned to Forrester's eyes. As he struggled to his feet, he looked above him as the last of the mist dissolved. His rage turned to panic, "I will not be denied again!"

With astonishing speed and agility, he drew his ceremonial sword from the sheath and with a lightening quick stroke, neatly severed her head from her body. As it hit the ground, it rolled into the embers of the still smouldering ashes.

"It's still not too late" he ranted as he grabbed the leg of the convulsing and twitching corpse lying crumpled by his feet. The blood formed a jet-black pool as it oozed into the darkened ground. He started to drag it towards the spot intended for Emma.

"No… not too late... this sacrifice will do… this will complete the circle." His ramblings became more agitated as he dragged and heaved the body along the ground.

But it *was* too late, for as soon as her head had rolled into the ashes, the flames released from the hidden force that had dowsed them rekindled with incredible speed and ferocity – so much so that Sam had to back away from the flames and shield his face. Forrester had reached the end of the road, however, for at the same time her torso, as if still attached to her head, caught fire. Unnatural forces were at work. The trail of dark, rich blood ignited and the flames rose from the ground and took the shape of a human figure – a female figure with curves and the long, striking hairstyle now so familiar to him. It bore down on Forrester, and within a second, his robes were alight as well. The flames spread and licked at the garment with such speed and intensity, he never stood a chance. In a grotesque parody of the dancing maidens, he staggered, twitched, and then writhed and screamed helplessly, before he fell to the ground in a crumpled heap. Within seconds nothing was left except for a pile of smoke and ash.

All fell silent again aside from the crackling of the wood in the newly rekindled fire. Sam was alone. Feeling bewildered and sick, his tired mind tried to take in the awful events that he had witnessed, but it was no use. After a few moments, he summoned his last remaining strength and somehow made the long walk back to Emma's car.

18

From the distance, the outline of the inn owned by the dead man, Hobson, could be seen through the greyness of the dawn. Its dingy light still shone from the foyer and Sam could see it even though it was still far away along the now familiar road that cut through the fells. He was heading there for no particular purpose other than a feeling that it was some kind of last outpost at the edge of the world – somewhere that no one could disturb him – sanctuary in fact.

The building was completely deserted and the door unlocked, now that all its occupants lay dead on the hill, and the rusty sign marked 'No Vacancies' and 'Druids Circle: One mile' still squeaked in the barely perceptible chilly breeze.

He staggered inside and climbed the stairs. He had a strong compulsion to dispel the stench of smoke and sweat engrained in his clothes and skin pores, and he made for the bathroom at the end of the corridor. An old fashioned bathtub with a deep base beckoned him. As he turned the cross-shaped handles of the taps, the expected clank and tapping echoed from the hidden pipes, but to his relief the gushing water soon turned hot and steam filled the chamber. He stripped and prepared for a long soak.

The warmth of the water enveloped him and he

breathed in the soothing warmth of the vapour. The steady and rhythmic dripping of the tap coincided with his breathing as it slowed and, as he stared at the light bulb above him, his eyelids grew heavy. The echoing of the dripping noise became louder.

He had no idea when, perhaps it was an hour, a minute maybe, or even just a moment, but the white disc of the shining bulb became pale, like the disc of a full moon; it shone through his closed eyelids. Then a pair of eyes and a mouth formed, so that he recognised the face; it belonged to Megan. She never spoke and her lips never moved, but she was talking to him through thought – from the other side of the psychic plain. He knew that. He could feel those thoughts returning to the dreams and visions he had when he was an infant, and they played before him again. But this time there was no angst, only a feeling that all had been resolved. He no longer feared them; the tower, the heavy ticking of the clock, the raven and that sickly fragrant smell, and above all, the megaliths and the many whispering voices emanating from them.

And, with the demons that had haunted him now done with and resolved, he felt warm and secure as he sank deeper into stillness, and darkness and a silently tranquil domain…

A sudden pain shot into his face and sinuses and he felt himself kicking out uselessly into the air. An overwhelming urge to cough and expel mucus shook him, and he sat upright with a jolt. As he continued to cough, he managed to laugh at himself. What a stupid thing to do – to fall asleep and drown in a bath, after all that he had been through!

He rubbed himself down with a towel and made his way to the room that Emma had occupied, and there he drew back the bedclothes and collapsed into them. This time he fell into a deep and dreamless sleep.

***

It was the sound of a lorry passing by that eventually woke him. He dressed and looked at the clock in the foyer. It was one in the afternoon! His mind felt clear and his limbs and muscles no longer ached, but boy was he hungry.

He made sure the door was locked and there were no lights still blazing, or any tell-tale signs that the building was occupied, and then he made his way to the kitchen. He ransacked the cupboards and the refrigerator and found eggs, bacon, sausages – just about everything he wished for. Then he turned on the stove.

As he sat down in the bar and ate his hearty meal, he could feel both his mental and physical strength returning – along with his spirituality. He remembered the seven principles of his faith, in particular personal responsibility and survival beyond death, and it comforted him. Emma was not dead, she had just moved on to the next existence, and therefore one day they would be reunited. There was no need to be frightened about moving on. It had taken Megan's psychic contact in his dream last night to remind him of that. But what about personal responsibility? Well justice had been served on the perpetrators, so that now all he had to do was find her mortal remains and put them to rest.

For a moment, he stopped eating and stared at his food blankly. Poor Emma. What, after all, if his beliefs were just some sort of fool's paradise and merely a false source of comfort? A lump formed in his throat and he hoped that when her last moment came, just like her fellow victims from antiquity she was sufficiently doped up with drugs and narcotic substances to be unaware of her last experiences here on earth. He shook his head and tried to dismiss this last encroaching thought.

But then he thought about Megan once more, and wondered whether there was more to the dream last night than merely a reminder of his faith. Then it hit him like a newfound revelation. He banged his fist on the table in triumph when he realised that for all of his life, he had overlooked the obvious. She was his spirit guide – Megan had been there since infancy – the strange woman with the hair worn long and in ringlets residing in his dreams, even way back then. Of course, everyone has one; mediums such as him use them to communicate with the spirits. His comrades had talked about them, but it had always been the same – the guides were always Comanche warriors, or Cistercian monks or such, and he had dismissed them as merely stereotypes and flights of fancy. But Megan? Well she was a spirit that dwelt in the stones – one of the oldest and original Daughters of Carrawburgh – more specifically, the Alnilam stone and one of the original wives of Mintaka, the founder of the clan. She had said herself that she was a vengeful spirit seeking retribution. Forrester, with all his over confidence and arrogance, had never bothered to question her origins and paid the ultimate price. Yes... Megan has been with him all of his life, providing guidance and stewardship during his time on this earth plain. It was all making sense, he just hadn't realised it until now.

After he had eaten his meal, he returned to the foyer and stepped behind the reception desk and into the small office hidden behind the curtain. He was searching for clues – anything that would lead him to the last resting place of his beloved. He rifled through the drawers, hurling them from the bureau and spilling the contents onto the floor. He sifted through receipt books and registers, before breaking open the cash till, and then proceeded to ransack the place out of sheer frustration over not finding anything. Without compunction, he pocketed the petty cash. The money, he decided, would be used for some kind of memoriam for the victims, and besides, it would be best if all of this looked like a common and opportunistic robbery. He did the same to the bar, and then the bedroom, but still he came up with nothing.

For a moment he sat on the edge of the bed and folded his arms in frustration over his failure. Maybe he was going about this in the wrong way. What would Megan do? Communicate with Emma of course, not dash around looking for physical clues on this plain. After all, Emma had tried to reach him on the night of the spiritual meeting at the Wychwood Inn, when he had chased her form into the graveyard.

Quickly, he dressed and set out for the stone circle again. That was the place to commune with her.

***

The fog had not returned and the sun burned bright in a cloudless, blue, winter sky. He paused for breath as he reached the embankment and surveyed the grim scene before him. Black ash and cinders covered the circle's interior as the last few wisps of smoke rose into the air. Its blackness turned opaque and luminescent as the yellow sun filtered through its billows – just like the morning mist, and it darkened the outline of the megaliths against the open sky. A smaller, separate and distinct pile of ash, the remains of which were once Forrester, scattered in the early evening breeze. But none of this fazed him, for he had purpose. The missing stone, the Alnilam stone as he now thought of it, had returned – and in the exact place where the charred remains of Megan's body lay. It stood there passive and innocuous in the sunlight, just like the rest, as though it had never left. He felt that it and the entity within – that is *she* – was watching him, still and silent now in her true form.

But what of Emma?

He could not sense her presence at all. Why couldn't he pick up on the spirit of the person that meant more to him than any other?

It was only then, when his recently renewed faith began to crumble again, that he realised that the answer was simple – her body wasn't there! He remembered from the night before how the Alnilam stone where Emma was supposed to lay remained dark and not a part of the psychic display. He could not recollect its shape, outline or anything…

As he looked to the sky, he realised that one of the plumes of smoke rising into the air was not a part of the scene in front of him; its source lay in the nearest of the foothills beyond. He strained his eyes, but then the sun lent him a hand when a golden ray cast and reflected onto the distant hillside. He was sure that he was looking upon a cluster of huts, or some kind of dwellings.

So he was not quite alone in this desolate wilderness after all. He recalled the words in Emma's diary that described the students and the Iron Age camp reconstruction, and he set off towards the hillside. They were her only friends during her final days – perhaps they could help him.

As he left the plateau where the stones brooded, the ground rose and a trackway came into view. It was new and fully ground out by tyre marks and footprints in the mud – a sure sign of people occupying the area. It led into woodland and, in his urgency, he stumbled twice and almost twisted his ankle, but he remained undeterred. The ground underfoot became steeper, but after what seemed like an eternity the track veered around a long and curving bend, and ended with a gate that barred his way. He scrambled over it and found himself in a large clearing. A scattering of large round houses of wicker and wood lay before him. Their vast, circular, cone-shaped roofs of thatch towered into the sky, and each one emitted a large plume of smoke from its centre. This was his destination; he had reached the settlement in the foothills.

He stopped in his tracks and surveyed the scene. No one appeared to be at home, yet as he took in the sight and sounds of the settlement, he realised that the students could not be far away. A small herd of goats bleated from a small fenced enclosure nearby, and a wooden rack containing unfired pottery stood opposite. Scattered on the ground were logs, tools and unwashed crockery – sure signs of recent human domestic activity. The smell of smoke, sawn timber and pigs filled his nostrils. Though late in the day, morning dew still soaked the ground in this sheltered clearing and added to the aura of calm. There was an air of hidden and undisturbed tranquillity all around him, with no sounds of humanity and machinery to puncture this serenity.

He headed towards the largest of the huts at the centre of the settlement, for it seemed the only thing to do. As he approached, someone appeared from behind the curve of the wattled single storey building. Any feeling of alarm Sam might have had was immediately quelled by the huge grin on the young man's face as he approached.

"Hey mate, look at the state of you, it must have been a hell of a party!"

This man, Sam concluded, was definitely not from the Iron Age, and he returned the smile and raised his hand as a greeting, realising that in spite of his newfound vigour, he must still look a pretty bedraggled sight.

The man acknowledged him, "Cool."

Sam's relief turned to anticipation as he crossed the threshold of the building and walked into the darkness. A movement within caught his eye, and only one thought occupied his mind. At the centre, a small human figure with its back turned, stooped over a stone hearth and fire. The heat of the room made him sweat, but as his eyes grew accustomed to the gloom, he could make out the figure's features. He knew it was a woman by her size and slight build. Beside her, a cauldron was suspended over the open fire, and she appeared to be stirring a ladle inside the hot, steam filled container. She was covered by a large, baggy shawl and hood, but her movements seemed strangely familiar to him.

Then he knew.

Was it his psychic gift or a sixth sense everyone possesses? It no longer mattered, as he walked towards her, his relief turned to euphoria. But by the same wonder, she knew as well, and as she stood and then turned around, she pulled down her hood. The long, soft, fair hair cascaded over her shoulder.

Her smile told him that she knew he would come, and they embraced. He tightened his grip, and he felt the softness of her body yield against his. Their lips touched, and her pale blue eyes moistened and they filled his senses. They were whole again.

"My darling, I thought you were dead, slaughtered by those evil –"

"Hush… hush now; it was important that Forrester thought that."

She cupped her hand around his jaw line and cheek and frowned as she looked into his pain and anguish. Then she smiled again with a look of devotion in her eyes.

"But Emm, I saw your spirit, I know I did… back in town at the inn – the night of psychic evening… I saw you go into the churchyard."

"Of course you did. That was me, but *real* me, no ghost. I wanted to be with you… I was trying to come to you, but when I saw Forrester in the crowd too, well I just ran. I had to get away from him."

He held her still more closely and kissed her forehead as he stroked her hair.

"Of course… of course. Forrester thought you were dead and a part of the ring around the circle, otherwise he wouldn't have dared go through with the ritual. And when he did, and the psychic ring collapsed because it was incomplete, it destroyed him. But how did you trick him into thinking that you were dead?"

She pulled away from the embrace, lowered her eyes and shuddered.

"That night they came for me, when I was trying to complete the diary, Gunter and Hobson were arguing. Hobson was nervous and jittery and trying to back out of it all and Gunter was out of his skull with booze. Then, Megan appeared out of nowhere and managed to persuade Gunter that she would 'terminate my life essence' as she put it. She would then take my body to the stone circle, where I presume it was to be burnt and interred."

He took her in his arms again. "She appeared out of nowhere? Maybe she was your spirit guide as well as mine."

"What? Anyway, she convinced Gunter to sleep it off, and then we left secretly. But we thought it best to leave my car at Hobson's inn to make it look as if I never got away. Eventually, I ended up here at the settlement among my student friends. I feel safe here."

Then she looked into his eyes with renewed intensity. "But my darling Sam, what you've been through... at the circle... it must have been awful."

"But you've been here. How could you possibly know all about that?"

"I know about it because Megan told me. She came here earlier, just before daybreak."

"But that's impossible... so you mean you don't know what happened to her?"

"What do you mean?"

Gently, he placed a finger on her lips to reassure her. For a brief moment, he thought of Megan again and felt sorrow when he thought how she had craved for the warmth of flesh and to be human, and not trapped for eternity in the coldness of stone.

"Like a ghost in the early morning mist…" he said, almost to himself.

Emma assumed he was referring to here and now. "Yes, it's peaceful here, isn't it?" and she gestured with her hand at the surroundings and the sounds of bird song filtering in from the woods.

"One last question Emm… the dream… I had a nightmare about you dying, and being driven and buried into the ground. I couldn't get to you…"

"Even people like you have nightmares when you're anxious and worried about someone."

"Or, maybe the souls of the living, in this case you Emm, can make contact with me through dreams, just like those of the departed."

"Mmm… yes, right!"

In spite of her mocking, a look of serene beauty and love flickered in the scientist's eyes.

They resumed their embrace, and without any more words, resolved that nothing would be allowed to part them.